THE BLESSED FRAGMENT

KAY HALL

For Pat,
God bless you.

Kay Hall
2020

WESTBOW
PRESS®
A DIVISION OF THOMAS NELSON
& ZONDERVAN

WestBow Press books may be ordered through booksellers or by contacting:

WestBow Press
A Division of Thomas Nelson & Zondervan
1663 Liberty Drive
Bloomington, IN 47403
www.westbowpress.com
1 (866) 928-1240

Scripture taken from the King James Version of the Bible.

ISBN: 978-1-9736-8513-5 (sc)
ISBN: 978-1-9736-8515-9 (hc)
ISBN: 978-1-9736-8514-2 (e)

Library of Congress Control Number: 2020902198

Print information available on the last page.

WestBow Press rev. date: 02/13/2020

Dedicated to

Davis Beasley
and the Beasley Family

The author acknowledges with grateful appreciation
her sister, Vicki Harshbarger,
the editor of this novel

CHAPTER 1

"WATCH OUT!" SHOUTED Nick. He was stunned and confused for a moment, but then knew beyond the shadow of a doubt that he was hearing the sound of gunshots. Afraid and disoriented, he saw the feminine shape in front of him fall to her knees. His instincts took over. Judging the direction the gunshots were coming from the best he could, he created a shield over her with his body, forgetting his own danger. He heard her terrified crying as his heart played a strong drumbeat in his chest, resounding loudly in his ears.

The gunshots echoed through the dimly-lit university student parking lot. Screeching tires followed, then silence. The danger was past for the moment. Nick helped the young lady up. "I believe the worst is over now," he said tentatively. "This must have to do with the police station across the street, maybe a police chase." Then he gasped as he saw that her leg was injured. "Your leg is hurt. Were you shot?"

"No, no," her voice trembled. "I must have hurt my knee when I fell."

"Well, at least we can be thankful for that." He noticed that she was blonde and blue-eyed, wishing he had responded more appropriately. He certainly wasn't glad that she had hurt her knee,

1

but the damage could have been much worse. Both of them could have been killed when the rounds found their resting places around them.

Sensing his dilemma, she made an effort to ease his embarrassment. "They say at church that we should be thankful in all things, maybe even for a hurt knee." They both laughed then, in relief that the danger was over. Nick saw for the first time the brilliant, engaging smile that was such a special part of this girl's beauty.

"I have told school administrators for years that we need more lights in this area around the university—I fought that battle while I was a student here, but I didn't get very far with my arguments. Maybe now they will listen to me," Nick said.

"Oh, so you went to school here too? I'm a piano major in the music department. That's why I'm here so late. We have piano exams next week and I wanted to practice my Bach pieces a few more times. Making high scores on those piano exams sure doesn't seem as important now."

"My office is across the street and down the block, so I often park here. I guess I should introduce myself. I'm Nicholas Danner. I was a journalism major here, and now I work for the *Atlanta Herald*."

"That must be so interesting, Nick. I'm glad to know my hero's name. I'm Patricia Noland. Not Pat for short, though. It's Trish. I'm very pleased to meet you, especially under these circumstances! That was a close call! I'm glad I wasn't alone."

"To tell you the truth, I don't feel much like a hero. I was scared myself! That was an experience I've never encountered before, and hope I never do again. As far as my work at the newspaper, I enjoy it. Right now I'm starting at the bottom of the pile, new guy on the block, waiting to get some real chances at my future Pulitzer Prize winning article. It would be a lot more interesting if the editor would give me an assignment that was exciting. Come to think of it, I will be checking out the story behind this with the police department! Who would believe that instead of covering exciting stories for the Herald, I almost become a front page story right here in the school parking lot!"

"I'm sure grateful that didn't happen. I'll bet you'll get your chance for a great assignment before too long. We all have to put in our dues. Remember, practice makes perfect," Trish said with a twinkle in her eyes, and they both laughed again. Trish was surprised how comfortable and safe she felt in the company of this striking young man. It was as if the harrowing experience they shared had created a bond between them.

Nick walked her to her car, hating to leave her, feeling as if he needed to continue to be there to protect her. Soon they reached her car in the parking lot, and they bid their goodbyes.

CHAPTER 2

THE RED CONVERTIBLE with its impeccable detailing, obviously meticulously cared for, stood out auspiciously in the front valet area of the five-star hotel. The owner and driver, Hammond James, closed the door to his second floor room and walked briskly down the marble atrium stairs. He walked with an air of confidence that attracted the attention of those around him. His errand for the moment was to make sure the proper arrangements had been made for the evening's tent meeting. Chairs, flowers, offering receptacles, his podium, and the flawlessly performing light, video and sound systems all had to be in place and ready before the first person arrived for the much publicized Hammond James Good News Revival.

His name wasn't really Hammond James. That just suited his purposes better than the name with which he was born. Ralph Jones. He snickered to himself as he thought of the discarded name, which he despised. Yes, Hammond James was a much better name for a famous revival preacher and evangelist.

He was a figure that turned heads as he ceremoniously opened the car door and climbed into the driver's seat of the BMW convertible. He was blessed with a shock of natural blonde hair that was appealing when all combed and ready for the revival meetings. He found it was equally inviting to those of the female gender when it was mussed. He was tall and muscular and did what it took to keep himself in excellent physical shape. He instinctively knew that was an asset in his chosen vocation. His hypnotic blue eyes that saw right into women's hearts made it difficult for anyone, male or female, to turn away from him. His teeth were perfectly capped pearls.

He wore his favorite white suit and tie. He had several sets of this ensemble. People liked this look, as it gave him somewhat of the appearance of an angel. But Hammond was anything but an angel--unless perhaps an angel of light thrown out of heaven as had been written about long ago. With platitudes and warmth that mesmerized his audiences at his nightly tent revivals, he would exclaim, "Give, give to the Lord!" and dear old ladies would empty out their savings accounts to fill his coffers. Hammond looked into the rearview mirror, put his foot on the accelerator, and sped out of the hotel.

A few days earlier, student Kathleen Evans had been hurrying across the campus to her professor's office. On a high hill in the small town of Lorelei was nestled a small college with buildings of red brick and white Georgian columns. For many years it had been a school for women only. But in 1958, the administration felt it was time to make the college coeducational. It boasted an excellent pre-med program and music training that surpassed many of Georgia's larger colleges and universities.

Kathy, as she was known to her friends, was a perfectly proportioned young lady who knew she was at the prime of her life and made the most of it. Her long, naturally-curly auburn hair flowed down her back and was envied by her friends. She was enjoying her sophomore year at Georgia Eastern University as a psychology major. She liked trying to understand what made people tick, and she was more mature and introspective than most college students.

Her freshman year had been tough for her. She had grown up

in a loving home with a close-knit family of five, and she missed her mother's support and love. Kathy was one of a small group of young ladies at the college with strong values who were determined not to succumb to the lack of morals evident on the campus, about which her mother often spoke with disdain. Kathy was waiting for the future, to give herself to the man who would sweep her off her feet, as her mom would say. A petite five feet, four inches tall, she was an intelligent, attractive package of curiosity who seemed to delight in the whole world. She drank in the sky, the flowers, and the splendor of humankind, living her life in awe of the continuing revelations of a master creator. Behind her back, others at the school called her Pollyanna, but she didn't judge others, so she had many friends and acquaintances.

Kathleen loved to learn. She greatly admired her psychology professor, Dr. Bruce Louis. It was time to choose a fall project for his class, and she wanted to please him with her work. She gave much thought to what her subject should be. She did have one idea that appealed to her. She had made an appointment with Dr. Louis to talk about the project, and now on the appointed afternoon she hurried across the grounds and down the walkway so she would not be late. After exchanging pleasantries with her young professor, she took a seat in front of his desk in the neat, orderly office, and began to speak of her idea.

"Dr. Louis," Kathleen said tentatively, hoping he would be in favor of her plan, "I have an idea for a project that I want to discuss with you." The kind professor nodded his head in encouragement. He listened quietly and attentively as she shared her thoughts with him. "I have learned that a tent revival is coming to our town. I hear it is the largest one we have had here in many years or maybe ever." Kathleen paused thoughtfully before she continued. "I would like to interview the preacher headlining the revival and write about him. I'd like to find out what it is that leads a person to become an evangelist, and in particular an itinerant preacher going around from place to place, pitching a tent to draw in crowds nightly. I think this would be an interesting study in psychology. I believe his name is Hammond James. The meetings will begin in town in a few days. He is becoming rather famous. I don't know if I can get an appointment with him, but if I can get to him, would you think that would be a worthy project for our class assignment?"

The kind professor sat thoughtfully for a few moments considering her plan. The enthusiastic spirit of the girl was infectious. He wished he had more students like her. When he finally spoke he said, "Kathy, you have always done excellent work for me. If this is what you wish to research, I will approve it. It sounds like a fascinating study of human behavior to me."

Beaming her perfect smile, she said, "Thank you, professor. I really think it will be interesting and rewarding."

"I suggest you attend one of the services so that you will have a reference point to start with. Then perhaps you can reach Hammond James and get an appointment. If he asks for a reference, please have him call me if I can be helpful to you. You can also call me any time, as you move ahead with this."

"Yes sir," she said gratefully. "Thank you so much, Professor Louis."

He watched as her light, happy steps took her from the office. If he had a daughter, he would want her to be just like Kathleen. He had always been so busy and preoccupied with his work, there had been no time for a family. All dedication, that was Dr. Louis. Like other idealists, as a psychology professor and psychologist he wanted to change the world, to make it a better place; to take away some of the pain and grief that the human mind seemed to bring to bear on itself. He sighed deeply as his student disappeared around the corner of the building, and turned his attention back to the papers on his desk.

Kathy could hardly wait until the beginning day of the revival meeting. She was always busy with her studies, so the day came in a hurry. She searched through her closet to plan what she would wear. Perhaps she would get a chance to speak to Hammond this evening at the revival meeting, so she wanted to look her best. She chose her favorite light blue dress. She felt it complimented the violet color in her eyes. She looked at her watch for the fifth time. It was almost time to go. A taxi was on its way for her, so she hurried downstairs to wait impatiently in the front gathering room of her dormitory.

Hammond James, alias Ralph Jones, was happy that it was warm enough this September afternoon for him to drive with the convertible top down. As he drove through the streets of the picturesque town, anyone he passed by could not refrain from staring at this handsome figure in the stark white suit. He grinned. It pleased him to see curious face after face turn toward him. He laughed with pleasure and said aloud to the spirit of the air, "Now, this is the life."

After all, Hammond had worked hard to get to this point. When his brain child, Good News Revival, started over eight years ago, he set up a much smaller tent than he had now. He printed some signs, contacted local newspapers for paid advertising, and managed to raise a crowd in every backwater town in southern Georgia, gnats and all. He hoped those pesky things wouldn't be here in north Georgia. Hammond knew by now that people in the south were eager to gather and sing the old hymns of faith and hear a message of good news declared to them in loud and fervent tones. And the healings—those were the best part. Once those were added to his nightly program, there seemed to be no stopping him. It was easy to arrange. People were so eager, so gullible. He had a troupe of young want-to-be actors who didn't mind traveling with him from town to town. The pay was right.

The twins were his favorite. He was brilliant to think of that angle and the identical twins were eager to have the work. It was a perfect gig for them. One of the brothers had been crippled in a car wreck when he was a child. He was confined to a wheel chair. It was so easy for the brothers to exchange places behind a curtain and have the first one appear to be miraculously healed.

What cinched the show was inviting a local doctor to examine the crippled twin before the healing. "Ha," said the right reverend Hammond James aloud as he reached the revival field and carefully parked his car, "If they only knew."

Hammond came into the large tent to find that final arrangements were being made and things were shaping up just as he had ordered. A fan sat on every chair, donated by the local funeral home. He swore quietly to himself, and said aloud to the sultry air, "It's going to be another hot night."

Some of his crew gathered around, asking if they could do anything for him, but he waved them off. He just wanted to be by himself as long as he could. What was this strange paradox that gave him the desire to draw huge crowds to hear the sound of his voice, when what he really wanted was to stand on the granite outcropping of Stone Mountain and dare anyone to come within 50 feet of him? How could he yearn to have the people sing his praises and at the same time long to keep them at bay? Ah, but yes, they did bring their money with them, didn't they? Hammond smiled to himself and shook his head as if to clear out the murky cobwebs that were clouding his thoughts. He had to get ready for the service tonight.

The last hour ticked by and the crowds gathered. Old, young, and children were settled in the assembly area. Hammond's faithful band, playing keyboards, guitars, horns and drums warmed up the audience just like late night television hosts' bands. People were already clapping their hands. Some shouted hallelujahs and other joyful salutations of praise.

The hymns were sung, the prayers were prayed and people waited impatiently to hear and see the star attraction, Hammond James. No offerings had been taken yet. Hammond had learned that purses and pockets emptied much more generously after he had spoken. But there was more to come before the major discourse of the evening. Hammond took his place behind the pulpit and seemed ready to begin. But a scuffle was heard in the audience.

Suddenly a young girl in a black dress stood up. "Oh, preacher, help me, help me," she screamed.

Hammond wore a surprised look on his face as he had rehearsed many times. "Come forward young lady, how can I help you?"

A well-dressed, gray-haired man took her by the arm and quietly led her forward. He walked with her up the platform stairs to where Hammond James stood now beside his pulpit. The young lady in black reached her hands and arms forward, pawing the empty air toward Hammond. "I am blind, I was born blind. Can you make me see?" The audience gasped at her words; the intake of their collective breaths was audible.

"Oh, my dear," said the trembling voice of the preacher. "Perhaps this *can* happen, with faith and prayer." Then he turned to his congregation. "What say you, good friends? Will you pray with me for the sight of this young girl?" The crowd came alive with shouts and claps and the cheers of a fine-tuned mob.

Hammond raised his arms above the crowd. As if by magic, they quieted to the last person. The only sound that remained was the gentle sobbing of elderly women into their lace handkerchiefs.

"Kneel, my child," Hammond commanded. The pitiful figure in the black dress dropped to her knees, making sure that the angle was the best for the audience to see. Hammond placed his left hand on her head, then his right over it. "Be healed of your blindness. Be healed. Be healed right now at this very moment," he spoke in his strongest, most authoritative voice. Even Hammond did not call on the name of God this time. Perhaps in the deepest recesses of his heart he was afraid that lightning might indeed strike him.

The young girl in the black dress gave a quiet moan and swayed in her kneeling place. She covered her eyes with her hands. Then she took her hands from her eyes, looked around in bewilderment and shouted, "I can see. Hallelujah, I can see!"

The grand chorus of cheers and hallelujahs broke out in the crowd again. It was as if they had all just been given the gift of sight. Hammond had worked the crowd into a frenzy of group-think, and he expertly took advantage of the gifts of empathy and compassion that are strong and steadfast in the human heart, waiting to be marshalled by the right person.

"Read from the Bible, let her read from the Bible," cried a voice from the third row, right on cue. Hammond could always trust Larry to break in with just the right comment at just the right moment.

Hammond nodded and raised his hand to the audience for quiet. He took his Bible and opened it for the young lady in black. She took the book, but she did not need to look at the words. She had recited them many times before in just such a scenario. Haltingly the words rolled from her lips to the ears of the crowd, "Blessed are those who hear the word of God and obey it. Luke 11:28."

The crowd cheered in agreement again as they watched the young lady in black return the Holy Book to Hammond and be escorted to her seat with steps as light as a ballerina. When the people had returned their undivided attention to Hammond, he stationed himself at his pulpit again.

"Beloved friends, what a joy it is to be here with you and with God. I can feel His mighty presence," began Hammond, with a special stretching out and strong vibrato on the word "feel" when he spoke it. "Here, here is the blessed word of God, our Holy Book," he shouted, holding it high as shouts of Amen were heard all around about him.

"I know you have your Bible with you, so turn with me to our text, and such an important text it is, my friends. Turn to Chapter 10 of Mark; you probably know it well, being the God-fearing people you are."

"Yes, yes," the crowd responded.

"You remember the story. A prominent citizen asked Jesus, 'Teacher, how can I be saved?' and Jesus answered him by saying, 'You know what the commandments are, but you need to do one more thing. The Bible says in Mark 10: 17 – 22, it's written right here, brothers and sisters, sell all you have and give away the money and you will have riches in heaven. But the man was very rich and he wouldn't do what Jesus said."

The crowd was very quiet now in their seats, the only movement the swaying back and forth of the funeral home donated fans. "Oh, my children," spoke Hammond, with a tone of great warning in his voice, "Do not be like this man who would not obey Jesus. Give, give all you can. God will bless you a thousand times over."

The ushers took their places for this important part of the service. The pianist played a rendition of *"Amazing Grace,"* changing the third verse, "Through many dangers toils and snares" to a minor key, then returning to the major key for the beloved last verse, "When we've been there ten thousand years." The audience sang with great gusto.

Hammond loved this part of the service best. But tonight his attention wavered. His eyes had been drawn earlier to a lovely young girl walking through the tent in a light blue dress who now sat near the back of the tent. Her exquisite, upturned face and her rapt attention fascinated him. He was startled at how much she resembled the angel painting by Leon Francois Comerre that some ardent worshiper had given him. He always had a gift for discerning the innocents, and ways to attract them to his charms.

Reluctantly, he returned his attention to his other followers. "Thank you, thank you for giving. It is what God wishes you to do." The fiasco continued, and many life savings were given away that evening before the last listener headed for home.

CHAPTER 3

WHEN KATHY REACHED her dormitory again, she hurried up the stairs, her small feet making gentle taps on the laminate floor. She was hoping her best college friend, Joni, was in their room. When she opened the door, Joni's voice rang out, "Hello, Kathy. Did you have a good time listening to the golden preacher tonight?"

"Oh, Joni, don't make fun. It was wonderful," said the breathless college girl. "I hope he will meet with me for my psychology class project."

"Hey, are you sure that is why you want to meet with him, Kathleen? You do seem to have stars in your eyes tonight," said her roommate with a bubbling laugh.

"Oh, stop," chided Kathy. She paused for a pensive moment, then confided to her good friend, "I do think he is quite a splendid figure in that white suit. You come with me next time, Joni."

"Oh, no you don't. You know I don't go for all that churchy stuff. God's a good guy and all, but I do fine without all those religious trappings," Joni answered.

"Well, I'm sorry you feel that way, Joni. But I love you to pieces anyway," Kathy answered. She put her arms around her roommate and gave her a hug. She was filled with excitement and anticipation as she thought of meeting with Hammond James in the future.

Joni returned Kathy's hug, but a shiver came over her for no apparent reason. She shook the feeling off, for her friend was so happy tonight, she didn't want to do anything to spoil it.

Bright and early on Monday morning, the next day that classes were held, Kathleen knocked once more on Professor Louis's office. He was delighted to see her at his door and opened it wide. "I hope I am not disturbing you, Dr. Louis," said Kathleen apologetically. "I should have made an appointment, but I was anxious to see you about my project."

"Come in, Kathleen. I have a few minutes before class. What can I do for you this morning?" he asked.

"Dr. Louis, I went to hear the preacher I was telling you about, Hammond James. I went to his revival service. I am interested in meeting with him, but I don't think there is a chance of that unless perhaps you contact him for me. Would you consider doing that, sir?"

The earnestness in her voice made her seem to be almost pleading. He paused to think on her request, but not for long. It would be hard to deny this lovely creature much of anything. "Why, yes, I will contact him if you wish, Kathy. Find out where I can reach him, will you?"

"Oh, I already, have, sir. He is at the Hilltop Suites in town. I'm sure they would deliver a message for you." A frown appeared on Dr. Louis's face, but he said with some concern in his voice, "When would you like to meet with him, Kathleen?"

"I will arrange my classes so that I can meet him whenever he is available. I know he has services each night this week, so perhaps one afternoon soon while he is still in town for revival services."

"I will contact him and get back to you, Kathleen. I have to agree, it may be better and more suitable if I arrange the meeting for you."

"Yes, sir, I thought that was best, too. I'll say goodbye now and thank you so much."

The vibrant girl was gone like a radiant butterfly that flew by in the garden flowers. The learned professor said aloud to the morning air, "I hope I'm doing the right thing." And he shook his head, needing the motion for his own benefit.

CHAPTER 4

PHIL DAWSON SAT in his swivel chair at his desk in the *Atlanta Herald* office. He loved that chair. It would turn all the way around. If he had a chance to be by himself and get away with it, he would twirl around like a kid at an old-fashioned soda fountain. Now in his fifties, with a great deal of experience behind him, he still struck a handsome figure. His hair was thinning, but his muscular body was still taut and in good condition. Phil spent six years in the Navy, and had learned good habits about staying fit. He loved life and he knew health was valuable. His wife, Sadie, scolded him lovingly each time she saw him with a donut or a cookie. "Well, why do you keep them in the house?" he would ask her, and she would remind him they were for the grandchildren.

Phil loved newspaper work. Long ago a wise teacher had praised him in his early school days, saying that his writing showed great talent. He never forgot that teacher's smile, or her words. During his service time, he attended college, compliments of the Navy. He studied writing and history. His professors recommended him highly to the *Atlanta Herald* when they inquired about his application, and he landed an entry level position. He received his first assignment and it was love at first write, for him and for his employers.

Sadie had given Phil two handsome, strong sons. He was proud of them, but neither had any interest in writing. One was a stockbroker and the other was a teacher and football coach.

Phil began to watch the new young man the *Herald* had hired recently. His name was Nick Danner. It seemed to Phil that he may have found a bit of a clone of himself in Nick, and that interested him. He wondered, was it his human nature that made him want to create another version of himself to help carry on the newspaper's future?

There was a polite knock on his office door and he realized that it was probably Danner. He had asked him to come to his office when he had a free moment. "Come in, Danner," called out the husky voice of Dawson.

"You wanted to see me, Mr. D?" asked Nick as he opened the office door. There was a mixture of anxiety and anticipation in the young man's question. The staff called Dawson "Mr. D." He was a fair man in all his dealings and his staff highly respected him. Phil liked hearing the abbreviated name. A secretary had given him the nickname years ago and it stuck. Nick wanted to please him with his work at the Herald.

"Come in, Danner, and have a seat," he directed Nick. He obliged his boss and sat down gingerly. Dawson sat quietly for a minute or two. He swiveled his chair to the right, then he swiveled it to the left. He looked the reporter squarely in the eyes while stroking his chin thoughtfully.

Nick held his breath until he finally realized he had to breathe. He thought his new boss would never speak to him. He sat quietly, wondering what was next.

"Nick," said Mr. D finally, "I know you have only been here a few months, but I have been watching you. You do good work."

"Th-thank you, Mr. D," stuttered Nick, still wondering what was to come.

"I want to give you your first big writing assignment if you are up to it."

Nick's eyes grew wide and bright and his heart beat fast in his chest. "I will certainly do my best for you, sir. That's great news. Tell me about it, sir," spoke Nick much faster than usual, his words tumbling over one another.

"Well, hold on there, young man, until you hear what I have to say." Nick knew it was time to close his mouth and listen. He took a deep breath and focused his full attention on Mr. D.

"Nick, we have many readers who attend evangelical churches in Atlanta and in all parts of Georgia, as well as many who are Jewish. Their sacred Christian days of Passover and Easter are coming up early next month. I wish we could find a new and fresh way to write for them, a new angle if I may use that word. I have arranged for you to take a trip to Jerusalem, to the Holy Land. I want you to observe the pilgrims there as they celebrate this special season."

Dawson paused for a moment, but Nick did not speak. He was feeling a bit light-headed and utterly astounded. Mr. D continued, "There is a great rift these days between the right and the left, the conservatives and the liberals. I feel we need to address the concerns and interests on both sides with our newspaper. In the newspaper business, it's certainly not our job to create the news, or editorialize on it. It's our job to report the facts and let our readers make their own decisions. Do you agree?" He looked at the young man seated across from him and noticed that his jaw had dropped and was hanging open.

He spoke again to help bring Nick back to reality. "Well, what do you say to that assignment? Would that interest you?"

Nick's jaw closed. He sat silently considering what he had just heard. "That's quite an assignment, Mr. D. I am proud you would even consider me for the job, but I have to ask, why would you choose me, sir? I am certainly not a religious person; in fact if the truth be told, I am an agnostic through and through."

"All the better, Nick. We want this experience to be written from both sides of the coin. I have been scrutinizing your work here at the paper. You are a talented writer, Nick, and you are objective. I need that kind of perspective on this article."

Suddenly the words of the kind teacher from long ago echoed in his mind and he smiled, for history does seem to repeat itself.

"Well, I will do my best, sir. I'm honored to be given the assignment, but just a little apprehensive if I tell the truth."

"I like the truth, son. The truth is just what I am after. I know you can do this. I will have Miss Johnson make the arrangements for you and let you know about them. Is next Monday okay? Hmmm...Monday to Thursday for your stay in the Holy Land, then back to write your article Friday and Saturday and we will feature it in the Religion Section on Easter Sunday." Mr. D beamed and felt very proud of himself for making this good plan. He walked around the desk to where Nick stood and gave him a gentle slap on the back as he left.

Nick closed the office door and stood stock still in the hallway. He was dumbfounded. He shook his head as if to clear it and headed for the breakroom. Maybe a cup of coffee would make him feel better. Then he was alone in the breakroom. The hot, black coffee tasted good and revived him. "My goodness," he whispered to the air. "I don't even know where to start."

Perhaps, although he certainly didn't intend them to be, his words were a prayer. For suddenly the pretty church girl came to his mind. He hoped her knee had not been seriously damaged that strange night at the university.

"Trish," he said aloud, making one of his co-workers who had joined him in the breakroom begin to look at him curiously. "Her name was Trish. I've got to find Trish. She could help me to at least get a perspective on all this. I have to find her if I can. I am totally out of my element with this religious stuff."

Nick didn't know where to begin in his search. He hardly knew her, and they had met for only brief moments. She had said she was a music student. She was practicing for a piano recital. He decided he would go to the music building at the university and see if he could be fortunate enough to find her again. He went back to his desk, grabbed his keys, and headed out the door.

He didn't forget to lean down as he hurried past Miss Johnson and tell her, "I have to go out on an important errand. My copy is already in. Back soon, Miss Johnson." She smiled at his boyish charm and happy countenance and jotted down his time leaving, just because she was supposed to do so.

Nick was soon at the steps of the music building of Atlanta University. He knew about this building. It once was the home of movie goers from all over Atlanta and was then called the Rialto Theatre. Nick went inside and soon heard a cacophony of music coming from the practice rooms. He heard the sounds of horns, of stringed instruments, of bell-like flutes, and of piano keyboards. Each room had a small window on the door to let in the light. Nick peered into each one in turn, hoping not to alarm or disturb the musician inside. "I will never be able to find her," said Nick to no one in particular. He would have said a prayer then, if he had been a praying man. He looked in one window, then another. Then, incredibly, he saw her sitting there at the piano. He caught his breath. He had forgotten how lovely she was, and after all, they met in the dark. He stared through the window as the strains of the Chopin Prelude drifted to his ears.

She played the final cadence, and her hands rested in her lap. Then she turned, as if somehow she knew someone was watching her. She was startled, but then she recognized his impish grin and was delighted. She had thought of him more than once over these past days and she had been wishing the forces of the universe might bring them together again.

Trish jumped up from the piano bench and opened the door. She put her finger to her lips to motion for him to be quiet and she stepped into the hall to meet him.

"Uh, Trish, hello there," he said awkwardly. "I was hoping I would find you here." Then not knowing what else to say he asked, "Oh, how is your knee?"

Her soft laughter made a sweet bubbling sound as she answered, "My knee is fine, Nick. See, the scab is all gone. Thank you for asking."

"Oh, you remembered my name. I'm so glad." A smile enhanced his already handsome face. "Uh, are you very busy? Are you thirsty? Could we go and get a drink?"

"Sure, Nick. We have a student lounge down the hall. We can get something there. And yes, I am thirsty." And they both laughed as if their conversation were more clever than it really was.

Soon they were seated together sipping soft drinks in the student lounge. Trish felt his shyness and awkwardness and wanted to put him at ease. She said earnestly, "Nick, I don't know you very well, but you seem to have something on your mind. I promise you, I am a good listener. I can be a good friend, if you will let me be. I would like that."

"Ah, Trish, you've got me pegged. I am excited about a writing assignment I just received from my editor at the paper, but I'm worried, too. Maybe you can help, if you are willing."

"I will share anything I can that will be of benefit to you, Nick," said Trish with sincere and unfeigned interest.

"Trish, we were just together for a few minutes at our first meeting; but you said something about church, I think. If you don't mind my directness, are you a religious person? Do you go to church?"

"Yes, Nick. I do go to church regularly. I have grown up my whole life in the Christian faith. It is a most important and meaningful part of my life, my philosophy as it were."

"Okay, then. I will just blurt this out. My newspaper, the *Atlanta Herald*, is sending me to the Holy Land next week to view the Passover and Easter customs there. I am assigned to write the Easter Sunday feature story for the religious section, and I am scared to death. I know next to nothing about the Christian religion. I hope I won't offend you, this early in the game, but I have always viewed all that religious stuff on a par with Grimm's Fairy Tales."

Trish was silent and thoughtful. When she finally spoke, she reached boldly across the table and took Nick's hand in hers. It seemed the right thing to do. Her eyes captured Nick's eyes and held them fast, as with an invisible thread that could not be broken. "Thank you for being honest with me, Nick. I'm sorry to hear that you feel that way, but I do understand. What a privilege you have been given, to see the Holy Land for yourself. That is something I have always hoped to be able to do; to really walk in the paths where Jesus, the one who guides my life, walked when he was on earth."

Nick listened to her intently, but he was at a loss. He had no reference point for what he heard her saying. He knew nothing of this Jesus of whom she spoke, except that he loomed large as a religious figure. He wanted this new assignment, but how would he ever manage to write a fitting article for his newspaper? Trish heard him breathe a deep sigh.

Trish was aware of his anguish and confusion as she continued to speak to him. "Even knowing how you feel, Nick, I am still willing to help you with the article in any way I can. Please excuse me if I sound dramatic, but I feel deep in my spirit that some destiny has brought us together. Go on your journey. We will meet when you are home again, and I will help you with the article if you still feel you need me. One thing I do need to explain to you. As Christians, we believe that Jesus was fully human, just like you and me, yet he was God, in the same flesh. It may help if you can go into this as open minded as possible, and ask God to help you to learn about the man…and the God…Jesus."

He held her hand so tightly and urgently that it hurt, but Trish didn't mind. A strong bond had developed between them in a short time. "Thank you, Trish, thank you," the young reporter whispered from somewhere deep inside himself. He seemed to relax then, and in a lighter tone he said to her, "Again I will have to say, I'm glad you skinned your knee that day." And they both laughed and the tension was broken.

CHAPTER 5

IT WAS GOOD to be with Trish, but Nick didn't have much time with her again before his trip. He spent every spare moment he had researching the Holy Land. He read everything he could find about Jerusalem. He wanted to be as prepared as he could.

The sun rose and set a minimum of times and Nick was standing at the check-in counter of Delta overseas flights. His flight would take him first to New York, then on to Tel Aviv. He had learned from the schedule that the flight would be about 10 and a half hours total. He could use the flight time to learn even more about Jerusalem.

"Well, here we go," he whispered aloud. He hoped that Mr. D had not been wrong about him. He wanted desperately to bring him a superb piece of writing. He wanted to reward the confidence Mr. D had placed in him. He wanted to please him with his work at the *Herald*. He headed for the security gates.

Just at the last moment before he entered the secure area, he heard his name being called by a sweet voice he remembered. "Nick!" she called out to him. It was Trish. She came to him, gave him a gentle hug and said, "I wanted you to have this to take with you." She pressed a small, black leather-bound book into his hand. He hurriedly put it in his right pants pocket and told her, "I have to go, but I will see you when I get home." He didn't want to leave her, but the flight would wait for no one. He smiled, waved goodbye to her and entered the security lines.

He thought about her on his flight to New York. He was surprised that she came to the airport to see him off. Soon he was on the second and longest leg of his trip. His computer was on his lap. He tried to work, but the screen often seemed to conjure up the face of a blue-eyed music student.

After a few hours of sleep, Nick awoke to find that the hours of flying time passed without incident. Nick was just one hour from his destination. He suddenly remembered the small book she had given him. The seat belt sign was off, so he was able to raise his body from his seat and reach into his pocket. He retrieved the leather-bound book from its hiding place. He read the print on the front, tracing his fingers over the embossed gold on the cover which read "New Testament," and learned on the first inside pages that it was a New King James Version of the New Testament. He opened the cover, and saw the petite, lacy, handwritten inscription from Trish. It said, "To Nick. May you find all that you are seeking and may God bless you in your search. Love, Trish." It was dated so that he might remember this day and this special trip.

He stared at the page. He took in the words. He uttered under his breath, "God bless me? Why should he? I don't even believe." He was curious about what might be inside, and couldn't resist opening the small epistle to the place where Trish had carefully placed a black silk ribbon bookmark with the words on it written in gold. He read the words she had chosen for him: "In the beginning was the word; and the word was with God, and the word was God," John 1:1 New Revised King James version.

Just then the seat belt sign came on, the bell sounds rang and the captain announced that it was time for passengers to prepare for the imminent landing in Tel Aviv. He would have to continue his reading at a later time. He closed the little book and returned it hurriedly to his pants pocket. In a very short time, the Delta jet was lined up with the runway lights about to touch down. Nick felt the plane meet the runway pavement as he landed safely in Tel Aviv.

CHAPTER 6

TWO DAYS HAD passed since Nick's arrival in Jerusalem. He was growing more weary, and more overwhelmed, with each passing hour. His computer was filled with details he had learned about the interesting, multi-cultural city. His head hurt from trying to remember so much that he had seen and heard. He was hungry.

He climbed into his taxi and spoke to his guide and driver. Yehuda had been a real find for him; he had been an enormous help to Nick. "I guess we will head back to our hotel now, Yehuda. I think I have all the information I need from what I have seen and heard." The clouds were beginning to take on a rosy glow in the western Jerusalem sky. Nick noted that it was quite a breath-taking sight. He suddenly thought of Trish, and wished that she was sharing the view with him.

Yehuda started the engine and Nick settled back in his seat. The taxi window on Yehuda's left was open. Suddenly a flying object came through the window and smacked him in the side of his face. Nick heard him yell, "Ow, metutam!" He slammed on the taxi brakes; fortunately there was no car behind him. Yehuda held his hand up to the side of his face. Then his attitude changed; he laughed softly and spoke to his passenger. "So sorry, Nick. I just saw a young Palestinian boy disappear around the corner. He must have wanted you to have one of the delicious oranges from this part of town. He threw it, and it flew through my window and smacked me in the face." Yehuda laughed again with good humor. It was contagious, and Nick joined with him. The laughter seemed to revive both of the men.

They started off again for the King David Hotel. Nick had seen so much. But still something nagged at the back of his mind; he felt he had missed something important. He spoke to his guide. "Yehuda, could I ask you about a subject that came up in my research, something about the 'place of the skull'? We haven't been there, have we?"

"That is an important place for the Christian pilgrims, but it is outside the city. Our meters cannot run there, and I did not feel you wanted to go out that far."

Nick reached out and put his hand on Yehuda's shoulder. "I feel impressed that I do need to go there, Yehuda. Could we make some kind of special arrangements? A fee for your trip? I am willing to pay what you ask. My editor would want me to see everything that would be pertinent to my story."

Yehuda had grown fond of this friendly young man in the time they had spent together. He did not want to disappoint him, but he was growing tired. He wished for this day's drive to be over so that he could return home to his family. "I'm sorry, sir, but my trips just do not extend that far," he told Nick.

"But you must take me, Yehuda," Nick heard himself plead, not exactly sure why this seemed so important to him. "I'll pay you double the regular fare. What do you say, friend? It is very important to me."

Yehuda gave a great, deep sigh. He did not want to continue this journey. But there are events in the universe which once set in motion cannot be stopped; and so Yehuda relented. "Very well, I will take you, Nick."

"Thanks, thanks so much, Yehuda," said Nick, earnestly feeling a great relief.

An almost reverent hushed taxi ride ensued. The taxi soon covered the few miles toward the place outside the city walls of Jerusalem. They reached Golgotha, called the Place of the Skull: the place of heinous executions suffered by guilty and innocent nearly 2000 years before.

"We are here," Yehuda told him as he brought the taxi to a stop. Nick stepped from the cab and stood looking at the craggy, rocky hillside that rose before him, now topped with trees. He turned to Yehuda and spoke only one word. He asked simply, "Jesus?" and Yehuda answered just as simply, "Yes."

Nick had no explanation, even for himself, as to what happened next. He was fascinated as he watched the Christian pilgrims start to climb among the gray and red rocks, reverently taking off their shoes and leaving them at the bottom of the hill. He heard quiet utterances of praise, hallelujahs and hosannas. The climbers paused along their walks to raise their hands in Yadah to almighty God. Their ardent faces were alive with devotion and reverence.

Caught up in the moment, with not even a thought for his safety as he climbed through the jagged rocks, Nick also removed his shoes. He felt no pain as he followed in the footsteps of the barefoot pilgrims. They climbed the sharp landscape together, all moving up as one entity. Up and up they climbed, until they stood together on a rather flat, but still rocky and tree-covered place. The pilgrims fell prostrate on their faces and cried tears of adoration. And Nick Danner watched in transfixed amazement, not daring to move from his spot on the rocky hill.

Nick continued to watch as this pageant unfolded before his eyes. Finally, one by one, the satiated worshipers rose and began to journey back down the hill. The hillside seemed bathed in an unspeakable joy and peace which emanated from the devoted worshipers. Nick was stunned. When only a handful of pilgrims still stood beside him, Nick broke his own silence and almost moaned as he said aloud, "Oh, if only I can find the words to record this spectacle for the newspaper. It would seem an impossible task."

After one last hushed moment standing at the bottom of the hill, Nick began his walk back to the place where Yehuda was waiting for him. He looked up at the storm clouds that had gathered above Golgotha, and decided he must leave this place soon. A long roll of thunder broke the silence. As he turned to go, he felt a sharp prick in the soft flesh underneath his right foot. It startled him and he winced in pain. Leaning, almost sitting, on the rocks, he balanced on one leg as best he could and picked up his right foot to examine it, but he could see nothing. He wondered if a viper could have bitten him, but when he looked at his foot there was no sign that indicated such a thing. He licked his index finger and gently passed it over the tender spot in his foot. Then he shrugged and placed both feet firmly back on the rocky ground and began to follow the last of the day's worshipers out to the cars that awaited them. He was limping as he went.

When Nick reached his taxi after stopping to retrieve his shoes and put them back on, Yehuda noticed that he was pale. He hurried to open the door for him. "You all right, Nick?" he asked, "You don't look so good."

"Yes, I'm fine, Yehuda. Let's go home."

CHAPTER 7

AFTER THE LONG flight home, Nick was anxious to get back to his desk at the newspaper. He located his car in the overnight parking lot and headed for the *Herald* offices. He just wanted to get down at least an outline of his thoughts. His head was filled with even more pictures than his camera had taken. He needn't have worried that he would not have enough pertinent information to write his feature. There was more than enough. He knew just what approach he would take. He would attempt to tell the viewpoint of the pilgrims he saw worshiping in Jerusalem and contrast it with the effect it had on a non-believer. It was a brave stance, but it should be interesting. It would be powerful, if he could find the right words.

Perhaps his mind was preoccupied at that moment as his car drove through the red stop light on Copeland Street. He knew the light would soon be green for him and he was in a hurry. The driver of the large truck coming perpendicular to him was just as preoccupied as Nick was, and in just as much of a hurry. There was a sickening noise of metal molecules crashing in on other metal molecules, and the damage was done.

Nick knew there had been a collision. His head was fairly clear, but he was in agony on his lower right side. He bit into his lip to keep from screaming. Mercifully, in the next moment he lost consciousness.

The shrill cry of sirens sang their wailing song in the streets. Ambulances and firetrucks raced to the scene, and rescue workers were soon busy. The strong and burley driver of the truck climbed from his cab. He was dizzy, but basically unhurt. Nick's car had been crushed from the impact and he was pinned in the car. The firemen immediately began to work with the jaws of life to cut through the side of the wrecked car to get to Nick. It took an hour to remove his broken body from the wreckage.

They pulled him free as gently as they could. His body was strapped on a long board prepared for this purpose, with special attention given to his neck to avoid possible paralysis due to his injuries; then the doors of the ambulance opened and he was lifted inside. Oxygen was administered and the ambulance headed swiftly for Graham Hospital emergency.

When he reached the hospital and entered emergency's triage, the staff was able to determine his identity from his wallet. It was in his left pants pocket. While it was spotted with Nick's blood, his papers were not beyond recognition. It was his right leg that had been so badly mangled in the accident.

The helpful staff found the emergency number of Nick's sister, Paula. They reached her in her class at Georgia Eastern University, where Paula was a pre-med student. She hurriedly told her teacher the situation and made her way to Graham Hospital as quickly and safely as she could.

She sat now in the waiting room, hungry for news of her brother. The doctor who would head up Nick's surgery emerged through the brown doors of the triage area. "Miss Danner, we are prepping your brother for surgery. I will need you to sign some papers to give us permission as his next of kin."

"How—how bad, Doctor?" asked the concerned sister. She was not prone to using many words, but got right to the point. Her voice trembled when she spoke.

The kind doctor's brow was furrowed as he answered her. "I'm afraid we cannot save his right leg. It is beyond repair and we must amputate if he is to live. I'm sorry."

"I understand, doctor. I will sign the papers. Thank you. Please do all you can."

"Of course," the doctor said. "We will keep you posted during the operation."

Paula nodded and struggled to keep back her tears. She loved her brother very much. They only had each other now that both their parents had passed. He was so young, so full of his dreams of being a great writer. She sat down in a chair in the waiting room and placed her things on the floor beside her. Then she gave up, put her palms over her face and cried bitterly into them.

All was in readiness in surgery. Nick had been given the anesthesia required and was lying on a shiny metal operating table. The bottom of the table had separate sections, one for his right leg, another for his left. They were both stretched out equally. The surgeon examined Nick's leg with great scrutiny. He observed the severe damage just below the patient's knee. The bone had been crushed by the impact of the truck. The doctor gave an involuntary shudder. He had seen the results of many accidents in his medical career, but the challenge before him was of the gravest kind. He breathed a deep sigh, and then draped each leg separately under a light green sterile cloth to await the operation. Now both of Nick's legs lay side by side stretched out equally, perhaps for the last time. Underneath the drape which covered Nick's right leg, several external fixators had been placed in the correct spot to hold Nick's leg securely for the surgery. The pen with its purple ink was ready to place the medial and lateral markings on Nick's leg, to begin about 10 centimeters below his femur. This was needed to mark the skin flap that would cover the stump of Nick's severed leg. The scalpel and the radial bone saw each waited in its place for the operation; first the skin would be cut around the entire leg, then would come the careful severing of the nerves, and finally would come the cut through the bone. The apt assistants all took their places, fortunately all had been on duty and available. Nick's leg had previously been bathed in the iodine solution. They were ready to begin.

The surgery nurse reached out to remove the light green sterile covering that was draped over Nick's right leg. The material fell away into her hands, and Nick's leg was visible to her. She was puzzled and startled. "Doctor," she said into the quiet room. "Doctor, is this the correct leg? It is tagged, but I am wondering…"

The learned surgeon studied what he saw. "What is going on? Check the other leg, will you? Maybe someone marked the wrong one."

And from the left leg the green drape fell away as well. They stared with mouths gaping at what they saw. Both legs were perfectly healed and perfectly whole. There was no trace of any wound, not even a major scratch. "What is the meaning of this?" cried out the chief surgeon. Everyone in the room began to talk at once about what they saw before them. There was no denying it. It was real. It happened.

When the chief surgeon regained his composure, he went to speak to Nick's sister. When she saw his pale face and his surgery cap in his hand, she knew that something terrible had happened. She stood to wait for the doctor. He reached her and almost fell into a waiting room chair. "Please, do sit beside me, Miss Danner. I have something to tell you. It's good news, but I don't know how to begin. Your brother's leg, the massive wound…it disappeared before we ever began the surgery. I can't begin to explain it. His leg had an extremely critical wound, but when we unwrapped the drapes from his legs, we found it completely healed, no wound, no cuts, no injury at all, not even a scratch. There was nothing to operate on. I am not one to believe in miracles…but I certainly don't have an answer for what happened here. I saw the wounds myself, and I was certain the leg could not be saved."

Paula reeled with the shock of disbelief. Her eyes grew wide in her ashen face. It was hard to take in the surgeon's words. When they did sink in, she was overjoyed. She laughed out loud and hugged the surgeon and said, "I don't know how this came to be, but I am so glad it happened."

"Please Miss Danner, could you keep this under wraps until we can make some kind of investigation. That would be helpful to the hospital at this point. We don't really have all the facts yet, and there has to be some type of medical report."

"Why, yes, of course. Can I see my brother?"

"You can in a while. He will be in recovery until the anesthesia wears off. Then you can see him in his room. We want to keep him overnight for observation."

The confused and bewildered doctor walked away from the happy sister. As he went by the administration desk, he directed, "Please cancel any more surgery that is scheduled for me the rest of the day. I'm afraid I'm not feeling up to it."

"Will do, doctor," said the puzzled receptionist.

CHAPTER 8

NICK WAS TIRED after his long trip to Jerusalem, his car accident and the stress of quickly writing an article with all the facts correctly stated. Mr. D had been very pleased with his work, and felt it was time for Nick to take a short vacation to regroup. He did not want him to get burned out, a hazard of the reporting profession. When Nick turned into the driveway of the Wessex Hotel in the small town of Coral Beach, he felt great relief. He realized he needed a vacation. He only had the rest of Friday and Saturday and Sunday. He planned to leave early Monday morning to get back to Atlanta in order to get in some extra hours at his desk at the Herald. He loved his work. He was a born writer.

The next morning the white beach sands stretched out in front of Nick as he lay prone in his yellow, green and blue striped canvas lounge chair with his ankles crossed one over the other. On this sunny Saturday that he had anxiously waited for all week, the steady coming in and going out of the ocean was hypnotic. He rested. He could always unwind in this quiet place, his favorite place, and contemplate the mysterious events of his life that seemed to continue to multiply.

He opened one eye, squinted and looked at the beach. Family members dotted the sand. He saw many sand buckets and shovels and he watched as little feet ran up and down from the surf back to mother and father, where they would be safe.

Nick sat up suddenly in his beach chair, alarmed to hear a woman screaming. He soon realized the screams of terror were from a young mother just in front of him and to his right. She was standing over the body of a small boy, who looked to be about three years old. Nick reacted automatically and raced to her. The little boy's lips were frighteningly blue. Another couple was waving their arms wildly at the lifeguard who was about fifty yards down the beach. He was soon running toward them, wondering if they had seen a shark in the water.

Nick reached the young child and the mother before anyone else. She had not noticed the surf had come in closer to shore, leaving her child swallowing and breathing in water as the waves broke over him where he sat in the surf. Now he was lying limp on the sand as the water rushed over him. Nick picked up the tiny limp body and held it in his arms. He ran toward the lifeguard, hoping to close the distance between them as soon as possible. The mother ran behind him, screaming wildly, "My baby, my baby, please help him. God help him!"

Nick held the little boy tightly to his chest. Nick and the lifeguard were inches from each other when they heard the little boy cough. Salty brine spewed forth from the boy's mouth. The lifeguard took him from Nick's arms and laid him on the sand. He was unconscious, but he was breathing. The crowd that had gathered soon heard the roaring sound of the rescue sirens. He was taken to the hospital, and Nick didn't see him again; not that night, nor the next day before he left. But he knew. He knew the boy would live. A mother's prayer had been answered, but in a special way about which she knew nothing. But Nick wondered.

CHAPTER 9

NICK SAT IN the eleventh row of the Atlanta stadium. He was happy to have a pretty girl beside him. He was glad he had asked Trish to accompany him to this sixth game of the Atlanta Aces season. They were leading the LA Lions 6 to 2 in the eighth inning. It looked like they would be the winner this time. Nick was proud of his Atlanta team.

Joe Turner was up to bat. Everybody loved Turner. He was called the home run king of this team. But it wasn't just that. Joe had the reputation in Atlanta of helping and serving many people. He was known for mentoring kids, for serving in soup kitchens, and giving to the community in any way he could. The fans loved him.

Trish and Nick were watching intently. He liked it when something exciting happened in the game. She would jump up and squeeze his arm, and once she even hugged him when the Atlanta Aces hit a home run. They watched as the batter prepared for his next pitch. The pitcher seemed a little off today. He had already given the umpire the chance to yell "Ball two!" He wound up for the pitch. The ball seared the stadium air like a bullet from a gun. As the fans watched in horror, the missile thrown by the pitcher struck Turner just under his right brow. The crowd of enthusiasts saw him fall in a stupor to the ground. A concerned murmur came out from the crowd. Everything stopped dead still. The umpire was silent. He and the catcher moved quickly to assist the batter lying on the ground.

Turner didn't move at all. Suddenly the players came out of the dugout to gather around him, even though their training had taught them they should stay in their places. They could not help rushing out to check on their friend.

Suddenly the crowd became silent, as if in one accord. The prayers going up from many hearts around the stadium were palpable. Members of both teams as well as onlookers in the audience took off their caps and held them at their chests, heads bowed, eyes closed.

Trish was as stunned as everyone else. She didn't notice when Nick left her side. He raced down the few steps that led to the field. The security guards blocked his way when he reached the field. They held up their arms and tried to hold him back. They did not want a riot.

Nick didn't protest. He didn't say a word. But he looked deeply into the eyes of the security guards, gaining eye contact with each of them in turn. Their expressions changed. Their arms fell to their sides and they stepped aside for Nick. The players followed suit as if a silent voice told them to make way for Nick to get through to the prostrate player.

"I think it's too late for him," spoke the catcher. "He's gone." He removed his mask and dropped it on the ground.

Nick knelt on the field beside the hurt player. It was his right eye that had taken the brunt of the blow. His eye was beyond repair, and would never see again, but the internal damage behind his eye was Nick's concern. Gently the young reporter reached out to touch him as everyone watched spellbound. He covered the wound with his right hand. Then he placed his left hand over his right. The stretcher bearers were on hand by now, and they watched silently with the others, but made no attempt to interfere. They felt the ballplayer had breathed his last.

Nick's hands rested on the wound for three long minutes as the crowd and the players watched. It was strange that no one interrupted; no one objected. The scene seemed surreal, as if they were all suspended in time and space. No one dared to make a sound, lest the slender thread of hope be broken. For they did hope, their human hearts clinging to the promise of better things to come.

Nick removed his hands. The nearby Aces manager gasped, his mouth hanging open. "What?" declared the astonished catcher. "I can't believe what I am seeing."

The worried pitcher let his breath escape in a deep sigh of relief, and he fell to his knees. His heart, which had been beating nearly out of his chest, slowed its tempo. He cried unashamedly. For Joe Turner sat up and looked at the group around him with a clear but slightly dazed vision. His wound had disappeared. Nick helped Turner to his feet. The crowd in the stands went wild. They cheered. They cried. They danced. They cried some more.

Nick said to the Aces manager, "I need to slip out quietly. Can you help?"

The manager understood and nodded. "The pretty girl on the eleventh row behind home plate in the blue dress, can you bring her to me?" He motioned toward the stands and the manager located Trish. She was so lovely she stood out in the crowd. The security guards soon brought her to stand beside Nick. In the excitement of the moment all eyes were focused on Turner as he signaled to the crowd that he was okay. Nick and Trish slipped quickly away, and as they left the stadium they heard the umpire yell, "Play ball." All was well.

Nick soon had Trish safely buckled into the front seat of his car. He put his key in the ignition. His hands reached for the steering wheel and he shook his head as if to steady himself before he started the motor. His hand fell away from the key and he turned to look at Trish. Neither of them had spoken a word. Nick's head fell into his palms. He covered his eyes as tears of relief and exhaustion flowed through his hands.

"Nick," said the concerned young lady. "It's alright. You're okay. I can't say that I understand what is happening, but somehow you are able to help people. You are able to heal them."

"I didn't know what I was doing, Trish," said Nick, his voice husky and halting. "I just felt compelled to go to him. It's as if my actions are being directed by some unseen force."

"I'm glad you did go. I know you don't believe it yet, but I am becoming convinced that the ruler of the universe, the loving God I honor, has given you a special gift."

Nick didn't answer. He knew something strange was happening. But God? He didn't know God. There had been no dealings with God in his life, before fate came into his life. It all started with his trip to Jerusalem. He had wanted nothing to do with a God he didn't know, couldn't see or hear. A plea of anguish came up from his innermost being as he cried, "Help me, will you, Trish?"

"Yes, Nick, of course I will," answered the dear friend who sat beside him, as tears ran down her face. She clung tightly to his hands. She loved him. She knew deep within herself that she loved him from the moment she interacted with him in a bullet-ridden parking lot.

He was able to start the car, and he drove into the spring night. When they arrived at her door and he said goodbye, she rewarded his bravery at the ball field. She stood on tiptoe and placed her warm mouth on his and kissed him tenderly.

CHAPTER 10

TRISH WAS FINDING it exciting to wake in the morning and feel a smile upon her lips. Every day as she awoke, her thoughts turned immediately to Nick. She yawned and stretched comfortably in her bed, but as she settled under the covers, her face took on a puzzled expression. What a mystery Nick was to her. She enjoyed attending the baseball game with him; but the crowds, stadium guards and the unexplainable situation frightened her. She remembered the comforting feeling of Nick's strong hand in hers as he guided her to safety.

Suddenly an idea made her sit up in bed. The early morning smile that had teased her lips became a full-fledged beam that lit up her face. "Oh, the concert," she said aloud as she threw back the covers of her ruffled bedspread and bounced to the side of her bed, her feet automatically reaching for her slippers.

"I wonder if Nick might want to go to the piano concert at the university," she said aloud to no one but herself.

Trish had many friends because of her kind and warm personality. Among the closest of these friends was Prin. Trish loved her name. It was unusual, and when she had been bold enough to ask her about the name, the answer bubbled up from her petite new friend. "Oh, Mom and Dad say they called me 'Princess' from their first sight of me, all red and squalling. 'Our beautiful little princess,' they cooed. It stuck and has never left me. Prin, short for Princess, get it?"

Trish laughed with her comrade with the golden hair and blue eyes, and she knew from the beginning that they would be fast friends.

Prin promised her several weeks ago that she would go with her to a visiting artist piano concert at the university. Prin was happy to join her, especially because it would give her a chance to see her brother Danny, who was a junior at the university. Prin had missed him during these last few years that took him away to college. They had so much fun together growing up as children. He had always been so attentive and loving to her. There had been no sibling rivalry between them, just a deep friendship through the years.

Danny seemed content enough at the school in the science department. He was a pre-med student and she was proud of him. A little twinge of worry about him had nagged at her lately. She could sense that there was something just not quite right with Danny. She decided he was just growing and changing. He was working hard at his studies. She wanted him to be happy.

Prin worked it out with Trish to make her trip to the concert a surprise for her brother. It was a delicious secret to savor that she would be dropping in on him unannounced. Trish had been kind enough to also invite Prin's parents to go with them. They would be utterly delighted to be able to visit with their only son.

Trish was anxious to call Nick and ask if he could attend the concert with her. She wanted to wait until evening to call him. She did not want to disturb him at his work at the newspaper. She got through her day studying music history, did her counterpoint assignment, practiced her Beethoven Sonata, and the hours passed. She timidly dialed the number he had given her, but with determination. "Hello, Nick. It's Trish." She was happy to hear the jaunty lilt in the husky, masculine voice she had come to love so much.

The invitation was given, and she was rewarded with a hearty yes from Nick. He may have been reticent to hear a piano concert, but with Trish, he knew anything would be a pleasure.

As Nick drove, the group chatted cheerfully. Nick insisted on driving, being the gentleman that he was.

It was the supper hour when they entered the circular drive at the university. Prin spoke up excitedly, "I'll bet Danny is at supper. Mom and Dad, shall we get a bite, too, before the concert? Is anyone hungry?"

"Always," answered Nick, and everyone laughed. He was a hearty eater, but burned the calories he consumed with his diligent work ethic.

The group entered the dining hall with Prin in the lead. She could hardly wait to see her brother. But after looking around the dining area, Prin said impatiently, "Hmm, he doesn't seem to be here right now. Do you see him, Mom and Dad? He must be in his room. He gets so involved with his studies that he forgets to eat sometimes. I know he needs some supper."

"That's a good idea, Prin," volunteered Trish. "Let's go to the dormitory and see if we can find him."

Nick agreed and they all headed for the dormitory. Upon arriving there, they found it uncharacteristically deserted and quiet. It seemed to have been left in its own care, just for this time at the supper hour.

"Mom and Dad, why don't you wait here in the lounge and I will go and knock on his door," Prin encouraged.

Danny and Prin's parents sat down in the lounge. "I'll go with you, Prin," said her friend, Trish. "Nick, will you come too, please? We need a male to yell 'women on the hall' for us." They all laughed, still in good spirits and anxious to see the absentee brother.

Prin knocked on Danny's door and called out, "Danny, it's

Prin. Are you there?" Once again her eagerness to see her brother
went unrewarded and her friends saw the joy on her face turn to
disappointment.

As they stood in the dormitory hall, pondering what to do
next, they heard a soft moaning coming from inside Danny's room.
They stood quietly, listening intently. "Danny, are you there?" the
sister asked again.

Prin looked anxiously at her friends, then reached for the door
knob. The door was unlocked. Prin opened the door cautiously.
What she witnessed inside the room horrified her, and her hand
flew to her mouth in surprise. She saw Danny lying on his stomach
on his bed, as he whimpered in pain. Prin and her friends took
in the scene. On the floor lay a leather belt with sharp hooks
and pieces of rock attached to it. Prin's eyes widened in horror
when she saw the marks on her brother's back. "Oh, Danny, what
happened?" cried the bewildered sister. "Who did this to you?
Who has beaten you, Danny?" Her voice trembled as she spoke.

Trish could wait no longer to intrude. She came close to Prin
and put her arm around her shoulder, holding tightly to her. "Prin,
don't touch him. I'm so sorry. We will call an ambulance. I will
get your parents." She hurried out the door to retrieve the waiting
parents and soon returned with them. The mother and father clung
tightly to each other as they took in the miserable scene.

It was Nick's turn to step up. He walked to Danny's bedside.
He was a strong man, but it almost made him wretch to see the
wounds in Danny's back. "Danny, can I help you? Will you tell
me what happened?" He had taken in the situation and with
discernment realized that Danny must have inflicted the wounds
himself. It would take some time for the girls to realize that this
had been self-flagellation. Danny groaned in pain as the girls held
tight to each other, their faces distraught with disbelief and angst.

With gentle help from Nick and a great effort of his own,
Danny managed to sit up on the side of his bed. His excruciating
pain hung on his face like a shroud as he looked into the faces of his

sister, his friend Trish, Nick and his parents. His gaze rested finally on Prin's face. Her tears flowed steadily now, and her body heaved with great sobs. "Danny, how can this be? I don't understand."

Nick interjected kindly, "Ladies, I think Danny may have done this to himself. Is that right, Danny?" Nick asked tentatively. Danny guiltily nodded yes.

"But why, my sweet brother?" implored Prin.

"I sin. God forgive me, I sin," the young man cried in anguish. "I have to pay."

"Oh, my dear brother, you could not have done anything so terrible. Are you a murderer? Are you someone I only thought I knew and loved for all these years? Nothing you have ever done could warrant such a punishment of yourself. You know that we believe that whatever wrong we do in this life, Jesus has already taken the punishment for us, as long as we know that this is true. No, Danny, you are good, you are so good." Her voice broke and she could say no more. She fell on her knees beside her brother and held him as close to her as she dared so as not to hurt him.

And then Nick saw it. It shone out as clear and distinguishable as the planet Venus in an early morning sky. Nick saw Danny's eyes rest adoringly on his sister and in his eyes was a blazing love. It was not the love of a brother for his little sister; it was rather the love of a man for a woman, a consuming passion that at that moment was evident for all to see. The brother reached out and put his hand on her bowed head and stroked her hair and moaned aloud again. "Oh, Prin, my darling Prin. I love you. I love you."

Danny's parents watched quietly. They were intelligent, discerning people and loved their son and daughter with a true and devoted love. Franklin, Danny's father, was not a hen-pecked man. He was shrewd and honest, and was assertive when the situation warranted him being so. Perhaps one loving weakness he did have was his fondness for Ellen, his wife. He was a devoted husband, and catered to her wishes most of the time. Though somewhat begrudgingly, he still seemed to bend to her will. It had always been so. But Franklin knew instinctively it would not be so this time. He could no longer stand quietly by. He took Ellen's hand firmly in his as he spoke with authority, raising his voice to her as he rarely did. "Ellen, tell them. We must tell them, Ellen."

"Oh, no, no. Please," she pleaded. He is our son, our baby boy." Her anguish was pitiful to see and hear as her thoughts battled with each other as if they were sharp-edged swords.

The room was dead silent as every eye was turned in the direction of Franklin and Ellen. Franklin took her face in his hands with great tenderness. He held her prisoner with his gaze, and she knew he had won. She nodded in assent.

The strong father turned his attention back to his son and spoke to him. "Danny, you are our dear son and we love you. You know that."

Danny was able to nod to his father in agreement. The pain in his heart was even greater than the pain in his torn flesh.

Franklin's voice continued as his son took in every word. "Danny, we need to tell you at last that you are our chosen son. Twenty years ago, we were overjoyed to give you a home that had echoed with emptiness because we had no children. No one ever knew. I had taken a new job in a new city. We kept your adoption a secret. We told no one. Your mother wanted it that way.

"You were our son. She wanted you to feel you were completely ours. I'm sorry, Danny, if that was not the right thing to do. We thought it was at the time."

Prin gasped aloud. She could not believe what she was hearing. It was very difficult to take it in. With a trembling voice she asked, "And what about me, mother? Daddy, will you tell me the truth? I want to know the truth."

The mother could not speak and Franklin answered his daughter's plea. "Prin, our little princess, you were born from your mother's body. We have heard doctors say it sometimes happens that way, that adoptive parents conceive their own child soon after bringing an adopted child into their home."

Turning back to his son, the father assured him, "Danny, we loved you both the same. Please believe me when I say that."

Danny was astonished. As he took in the remarkable words he heard, as they truly sank in, the pain from the wicked whelps on his back seemed to ease. Prin was not his sister. As the truth of this confession from his parents pierced his consciousness, his joy became unimaginable. Could this really be possible? Could he really be free to love Prin as he wanted, as he could not avoid any more than he could avoid breathing every breath? It seemed that the dead of winter had turned into a glorious spring for him in that moment. He loved her so.

Prin would need some time to adjust to this new situation. She had no idea of his deep feelings for her, as he had never allowed his feelings to lead to actions that would betray his heart. She was bewildered and confused as she tried to take it all in. She looked timidly at Danny, not ready as yet to respond to this new development. But her warm and loving heart was always open to new experiences, and she had great faith in God as her constant guide.

It was Nick's time now. His own spirit had been pricked as he heard Prin talk about forgiveness. He was beginning to understand the words he had read from the small testament Trish had given him just before his flight to the Holy Land. He would have to find more time for contemplating his thoughts at a later time. For now, he felt the call of healing in every fiber of his being. His rich, baritone voice gave the next direction to all of them. "Could I have some time alone with Danny, please?" His voice was not demanding, but it reached to the core of the mind and the heart of everyone listening. It was mystical. They filed silently from the room, leaving only Danny and Nick together. Prin shared a sweet, shy smile with Danny as she closed the door behind her.

They were alone. Nick walked to Danny's bedside. Something in Nick's manner assured Danny that he was not to be feared.

"Would you lie down again on your stomach, Danny." And the wounded subject did as Nick asked without a question.

Danny's back showed a wild, jagged design and years of repeated scarring in the skin of his strong, young back. He lay motionless on his bed. Nick's heart reeled with pity as he once again examined the stripes from the cruel hooks and pieces of metal. He did not want to add in even a small measure to Danny's pain. He reached out to touch him. He began to trace each wicked, screaming whelp with his finger. As he moved, his mind turned to the thought of the wounds of the one who carried a cross to Golgotha, which he learned about on his trip to Jerusalem. Nick's soul came to a place of understanding. Together, the two men rejoiced, as one by one the tears in Danny's back returned to normal. One by one, at Nick's touch, the miracle of healing danced on the wounds in Danny's back.

CHAPTER 11

HAMMOND JAMES WAS restless this particular Monday morning. He walked back and forth in his room at the Hilltop Suites, drinking a cup of hot, black coffee that room service had provided for him. Something nagged at his mind. He certainly should be content. He had filled the offering plates with a great deal of money this weekend, and there were still five more services to come. He sipped his coffee, and suddenly stopped dead still as he recalled the vision of the girl in the back row in the blue dress. He wished he could see her again.

The phone rang and took him out of his reverie. "Hammond James, here," said the evangelist into the phone.

"Mr. James, you have a message here at the desk if you wish to come by at your convenience."

"Right, thanks."

Glad to have an errand to break the monotony, Hammond took the elevator down to the hotel front desk. "You have a message for me, Hammond James?"

The courteous young man reached behind him and handed over a note drawn from the cubicles on the desk. Hammond walked away for privacy and read the message. "Dear Mr. James, I am the chairman of the Psychology Department at the university here in town. I have a student, Kathleen Evans, who would like to interview you for a class project. Would you be amenable to that? We would be grateful here at the university for your help to one of our students. Please contact me at 550-232-9949."

Hammond swore under his breath. "Something else to bug me and take what little free time I have. Still, good public relations, I guess. Might bring in the students from the university. Who knows, some of them may have wealthy parents." He heaved a sigh and took his cell phone from his pocket and called Dr. Louis's number and set up an appointment with the student.

Kathleen spotted her roommate, Joni, in the university cafeteria and waved excitedly to her. "Joni!" she called out and took her lunch tray to the table where Joni was seated. She laid her plate of vegetables on the table and sat down. "What's up, Kathy? You look like you just won the lottery. Hey, you didn't, did you?"

"No, silly, I didn't, but I did get an appointment with Hammond James, the revival preacher that I'm interviewing for my psychology course. Dr. Louis arranged it for me. I'm meeting with him tomorrow afternoon," she said with a smile a little too broad for the circumstance she was describing.

"Is he coming to the campus?" asked her thoughtful friend.

"Uh, no, I have to meet him where he is staying, Joni."

"You mean, at his hotel, Kathy?" asked Joni incredulously.

"Why, yes, Joni. Why are you looking at me like that? I'm sure we will meet in a hotel conference room. Don't be ridiculous—he is a man of God, a preacher, for goodness sake."

"Yeah, well, he's still a man. Tell you what. I think I will go with you. Is that okay?"

"I'm sure that would be fine. I would really like to have the company."

"Good. That makes me feel better," said Joni. "I'm probably just being over protective, but I care about my roomie." She gave Kathy a hug. "You can't be too careful, you know."

Kathy's classes dragged all day on Monday. She slept fitfully

Monday night in her dormitory room. She couldn't get her mind off Hammond and the coming meeting. She awoke very early and was surprised to hear soft groaning sounds coming from Joni's side of the room. She sat up in bed and spoke to her roommate. "Joni, are you okay, buddy?"

"Oh, yeah, don't worry, Kathy. It's probably just a headache."

Kathy went to Joni's bed and reached out to touch her forehead. "Good heavens, you are burning up. I know you must have a fever. We need to get you to a doctor."

The good friends dressed hurriedly and headed to the doctor's office. The doctor examined Joni gently. "You are the fifth student I have seen with this virus. It seems to be racing through the campus. I'm afraid I will need to keep you here for a couple of days until you feel better and until we know a little more about this virus." More groans were heard from Kathy's brunette, brown-eyed roommate. "Well, okay, if you say I have to stay," she said. Then she thought of Kathleen's planned visit with the evangelist.

"Oh, Kathy, your appointment with Hammond James! You will have to cancel it. You need me to be with you, as a chaperone."

"Oh, Joni, I always need you, but I can go alone. I would never get another appointment if I canceled this one. I have to get that interview for my class. Don't worry. I'll be fine." Her roommate clenched her jaw and was resigned to the fact that it just couldn't be helped.

Excited, although anxious, Kathy took a taxi that afternoon to her first encounter with the evangelist Hammond James. He was pleasantly surprised that the blonde he had singled out among the crowd at one of his previous tent revival services was the collegiate who had asked to interview him for her psychology class. Realizing he was performing Act 1 of a play that could continue according to the designs he might have for Kathy in the future, the evangelist politely provided just the right information she needed for her class. At the end of the interview, Hammond politely placed her into her taxi and bid her goodbye. He made a mental note of the groundwork he had to lay first before he would meet with her again. Next time, the evening would end differently, if he had anything to do about it.

CHAPTER 12

KATHY AND HER roommate were in the library studying together. They were such good friends and enjoyed doing things together as much as possible. Even though they were opposites in many ways, the friendship stuck hard and fast as soon as they had met at the small university. Perhaps it was happenstance that the two girls had been assigned to room together; but not if you asked Kathy. She had a strong belief that a guiding force in the universe led certain people together. Joni suddenly broke the stillness in their corner of the library. She was taking a break from her studying of medieval history and had picked up the daily newspaper. "Hey, Kathy," she whispered across the table, "Isn't this the guy that you interviewed last year for your psychology project? Wasn't his name Hammond James?"

Kathy looked up immediately from her book. "Let me see that, Joni," and she reached across the table and snatched the newspaper from her roommate. There in big bold print was the announcement of the services to be led by Hammond James again this year. There was also a large smiling, beguiling photo of the man she had interviewed last year. "This newspaper says that he will be in town all next week."

Kathy's keen interest made Joni laugh and say, "Hey, hold it there, girl. I didn't know you were that smitten with him."

Kathy made a conscious effort to curb her enthusiasm. "Oh, don't be silly, Joni. I did enjoy doing the project, though. Maybe we should go to the service. You missed meeting him last year, remember?"

"Oh, that's right. I didn't want you to meet with him without me."

"But it all turned out fine, didn't it?"

"Well, I guess so," said Joni hesitantly. Then she glanced at her watch and jumped up from her chair. "Oh no, I'm late for my next class." She gathered her belongings in her arms and headed for the library exit, waving to Kathy as she went.

Kathy sat quietly, still gazing at the angel-like photo of Hammond James in his all white suit. She would like to see him again, she admitted to herself.

She left the library and headed across the campus to her dorm room. It was a sunny day, but Kathy shivered as if a cold, foreboding wind had crossed her path.

Kathy returned to her busy schedule and soon forgot about Hammond James. The weekend came, and she was enjoying a relaxing break in her room when the dormitory telephone rang. She heard it in the hall but didn't pay much attention. The girls took turns answering it. There weren't many calls on the hall phone since the advent of cell phones. Just about everyone had a cell phone. She was surprised to hear a soft knock on her door and a voice say, "Kathy, phone call for you."

"Coming," said Kathy, and she walked down the hall, wondering who would be calling her on this phone, and picked up the receiver. "Hello?"

Her violet eyes grew wide when she heard the deep, sonorous voice say, "Hello, Kathy. This is Hammond James. Do you remember me? We met last year when I was here."

Y—yes", stuttered Kathy, struggling to regain her composure.

"Of course, I remember you, Rev. James. You were so kind to help me with my psychology project."

"Well, can I call in that favor, Kathy? It would be a great help to me if you and I could meet and talk about the folks who live in this area. I feel it would be of benefit for our services.

Perhaps we could meet for dinner this weekend if you are not too busy. They have a buffet at the Hilltop Suites that is quite delicious. Could you join me on Saturday evening, say about seven o'clock if that is not too late?"

Kathy took in a deep breath. She wished she had time to discuss this with Joni, but he was here on the telephone now, so she made a decision. "Why, yes, Rev. James. I think I can do that, if you are in need of my help, sir."

"Hey, not so formal there, Kathy. Please call me Hammond, if you don't mind."

"Yes. Hammond. Thank you for the invitation."

"Shall I pick you up a few minutes before seven? I will be in a red sports car."

"That will be fine. I will be in the student center watching for you."

"See you then," signed off the resonant voice of Hammond James. Kathy replaced the phone receiver and stood motionless in the hall. Then she said to no one in particular, "Oh my goodness, what will Joni say?" and she hurried back to her room.

Kathy fidgeted nervously in her room until Joni finally came in. Her roommate knew something was up, just by looking at Kathy. She didn't have to wonder for long. Kathy was bursting to tell her what had happened. "Joni! You won't believe what just happened."

"Whoa there, girl. Calm down and tell me."

"Hammond James called and asked me to go to dinner with him."

It took a minute for Joni to make the connection. "Hammond

James," she repeated. "You mean the revival preacher? The one we spoke about this week?"

"Yes, Joni. He said he needed my help getting to know about the people in our area before the services next week."

"Oh, he did, did he? Well, are you going? Do you think it is the right thing to do?"

"Well, yes, I guess so. He did seem sincere in asking for my help," she said.

"Hmm. Maybe. I'm thinking he just wants to be with you."

"Is that so bad, Joni? It's really kind of exciting. He is such an interesting person."

"Yeah, he's a colorful character all right. Just be careful. We don't really know him."

"Oh, it will be fine." Kathy seemed to brighten even more with a new idea. "I know, Joni, let's call Trish in Atlanta and invite her to come to visit next week. I haven't seen her in a while. We can all go to the revival services together. Perhaps her new friend Nick can bring her. I haven't had a chance to meet him. She talks about him all the time and seems to like him very much."

"Sounds like a plan, Kathy. Just be careful with all this," Joni said as she reached out and took Kathy's hand into hers. She loved her as though she were her sister, and wanted only the best for her.

CHAPTER 13

KATHY STOOD INSIDE the university student center waiting for Hammond James to arrive. She was excited and a bit over anxious, peering out the window watching for the red sports car. It had crossed her mind that the car was a rather strange vehicle for a preacher to be driving. She wanted to know about that from Hammond James. She wanted to know many things about Hammond that she did not know.

Joni sat with her and had mixed feelings. She was happy to see Kathy almost giddy over the prospect of meeting with Hammond, but worry nagged at her like the gnats that flew into south Georgia and just wouldn't go away.

"There he is," Kathy said to her good friend.

"Calm down," scolded Joni. "It's not the president of the United States, you know, or the winner of American Idol."

"Hmmmm…" Kathy waved her hand in the air toward Joni in a gesture that meant, "Oh, hush."

Kathy headed for the door of the student center. She knew that Hammond would have a hard time finding a parking place. She wanted to let him know she was there and ready to jump in the cardinal colored car. She waved at him, and he stopped the car, got out and came around to open the car door for Kathy. Her smile was radiant.

Joni was still watching from inside the student center and she said softly, "Well, that's one point for him. He seems to be a gentleman after all." She cocked her head to one side and a frown covered her face as she breathed a quiet prayer, "Please take care of her, Lord." She shrugged her shoulders and went back to her student center chair to finish her reading assignment for her next English class. Sometimes her young and beautiful English professor would come into class, ask the students three or four questions on the assignment, and if she felt the class had done the reading, she would dismiss them. Joni always wanted to be able to help bring that to pass. She breathed a deep sigh and opened her book. University time was precious. It seemed to Joni that there was never enough time to get everything done.

Kathy was also a very conscientious student, but for now, her schoolwork was the farthest thing from her mind. She sat in the car beside Hammond and answered his small talk questions about where she grew up and how school was going. She tried to be nonchalant and witty and not show her nervousness.

"I think you will enjoy the buffet this evening, Kathleen," said Hammond as they drove into the parking lot of the Hilltop Suites. "Maybe it will be a change from school food, anyway."

"Thank you, Hammond. I'm sure it will be delightful."

The dinner conversation was lively and flowing, and Kathy soon remembered that this man across the table from her had a gift for saying just the right thing. She was vaguely aware of a feeling as if she were on previous visits to the university theatre where she had caught some of the rehearsals of the works of Shakespeare and Tennessee Williams. Hammond James was definitely a charmer, as Joni would say.

As the charmer signed the bill for dinner, he surprised her when he said very casually, "Kathleen, I really enjoyed the interview with you when I was here last year. I have thought about you often as I traveled."

"Really?" said Kathy, somewhat taken aback.

"Yes, really," said the preacher as he reached across the table and took her hand in his.

She was speechless and could only gaze deeply into his ocean blue eyes.

Aware of her awkwardness, sadistically thrilled at her innocence, he ventured further. "Do you think we could have more of the interview time like we had before? There is so much more I want you to know. Is that something that would be useful again in your school studies?"

Kathy's head was beginning to spin. She wondered why she was so flustered, for she had not had any alcohol. Only the delicious southern sweet tea that she always enjoyed. It had been waiting on the table for her when she came back from the ladies room. She had vaguely noticed that the glass had been moved, but she thought nothing of it.

So she was being offered more time with this man who looked like a Greek god? What could that hurt? "Why, yes, I guess so, Hammond. I enjoyed our interview very much."

"Good. I was hoping you would say that. I have a lovely suite, the best in the hotel. Shall we go there? I really am anxious to talk with you, to let you know about my ministerial work."

A small voice whispered in her head; it sounded like Joni, saying, "Be careful, my friend." Her mind was flying in many different directions and that was not one of the frequencies that managed to get through, for very long, anyway. He took her hand in his as they left the restaurant and walked down the hallway.

"Come in, Kathleen," said Hammond as he opened the door to the expensive suite that was paid for by the offerings given generously by his devoted fans. "I think we can manage to be comfortable here."

"Oh, yes, thank you, Hammond," said the naïve girl, who

was feeling more dizzy-headed by the minute. "Can I—can I sit down, Hammond?"

"Of course, Kathleen." He sat down on the soft, plush couch, the color of elderberry wine, and patted the velvety space beside him. The Big Bad Wolf said to Little Red Riding Hood, "Come and sit beside me, sweet Kathleen."

Kathy took a few unsure steps and managed to reach the place Hammond had saved for her, and she sat, or almost fell, into the spot. His arms went around the lithe form beside him, and he kissed her. Kathy's body responded in a way that amazed her. It was as if fever suddenly raced through her veins.

All her inhibitions were gone; all virtuous teaching was forgotten. She was here in this magnificent place with the golden-haired preacher. She was confused, and was unknowingly in a drug-induced state. The beast in Hammond James took away her innocence as God, who gives all human beings free choice, could not interfere. The roofie that Hammond so expertly put in Kathy's drink would leave no remnants in her mind of the evening they had shared together. At the end of the evening, he drove her back to her school, and she walked into her dorm under her own power, none the wiser about what had occurred.

CHAPTER 14

KATHY WAS GLAD that Trish had decided to drive up from Atlanta with her friend, Nick, and attend the revival service with her. It was evident to her friends that she was very excited.

"Oh dear, we are late for the service, I'm afraid," said Kathy as they pulled into the only parking space they could find. They had quite a way to walk to reach the tent where the revival service was being held.

"Sorry, Kathy," said Trish. "We got here as soon as we could. The traffic was just impossible."

"Of course you did," responded Kathy sweetly.

Nick escorted them inside the makeshift place of worship and they managed to find three seats near the back. "Ladies," said Nick courteously as he pointed out the seats and waited for them to enter the back row, then joined them, somewhat begrudgingly. Nick felt scorn for this religious dogma, but he wanted to please Trish, so he was willing to do as she wished and drove her to the small college town to meet her friend, Kathy.

The pumped up crowd had just sung a rousing verse of "Blessed Be the Name." Now their eyes were glued to Hammond James for the next chapter of the evening. They came to worship God, but it was this tall figure dressed in white with the glistening smile that had their rapt attention. From the side of the tent a commotion was heard. A young man was suddenly pushed forward through the crowd in a wheelchair and the listeners heard a voice cry out, "Oh, help him. Please help my son." The mother pushed the wheelchair to the front, as close as possible to the platform on which Hammond James stood. Her pitiful cry of anguish touched many hearts who heard it.

"Yes, dear lady. What do you wish of me?" asked Hammond.

"I—I was hoping, I thought maybe you could heal my son. He has been crippled since his legs were crushed in a car accident." The woman appeared so distraught that she fell into a faint; one of Hammond's assistants caught her in his arms.

"A doctor—is there a doctor in the house? We invited Dr. Lou Andrews, one of your town's well- known doctors, to be here tonight. Is he here by any chance?" asked Hammond's second in command.

"Yes, I am here," spoke a shy voice in the crowd. Dr. Andrews made his way to the front. Several people spoke to him on his way. He was a respected doctor in this town. He was a church man, yes; but frankly very skeptical of tent meetings such as this. He went first to check on the woman who fainted. The crowd saw that she had recovered. They registered their approval with loud applause.

"Dr. Andrews, would you mind examining this crippled young man? Will you tell us about this poor, wounded soul?"

Dr. Andrews didn't say a word. He bent down to gently touch the young man's legs. He didn't like this predicament in which he found himself, but he didn't know how else he could respond without causing a scene. He stood again and spoke quietly, but with the authority that came from many years of doctoring. "The bones of this young man's legs have been crushed. I don't believe there is any possibility that he will ever walk again. I'm sorry." The kind doctor made his way back to his seat in the congregation. His duty had been done, and although he did not like being used in this fashion, he had told the truth based on his years of experience.

The crowd murmured in sympathy with the woman and her son. Hammond held the palms of his hands out toward them. "Friends, we will take care of them." To the assistants who were helping he said, loudly enough for the audience to hear, "Take them outside for a moment, refresh them with some water, and perhaps they will feel like joining us again." The mother rolled the wheelchair-bound boy out of sight, as a single strong voice in the crowd began to sing Rock of Ages and the congregation joined in. It all seemed so spontaneous. As the worshipers joyfully sang the last verse, their heads turned to watch as the mother rolled the wheelchair back in and took its place in the front row of worshipers. Their attention had waned; the boy in the wheelchair was no longer of interest to them.

"Friends, let us turn to God's word for direction and strength. It seems fitting to me that we read from the seventh chapter of Matthew, verses 7 and 8," boomed the voice of Hammond James, commanding the crowd's attention once again. "You have heard it many times before. The Holy word says 'Ask, and it shall be given you; seek and ye shall find; knock, and it shall be opened unto you; for every one that asks receives and he that seeks finds; and to him that knocks it shall be opened.'"

"Amen, yes, praise God," members of the crowd called out.

Then Hammond James surprised the crowd as he gave a loud, piercing groan and swayed in his pulpit.

"Oh how can we read this?" he shouted. "How can we hear these words and not believe them?" The crowd was confused, but hung on with ravenous hunger to his every word and move.

He suddenly moved away from his pulpit and jumped from the platform. He headed for the young man in the wheelchair, rolled him out and whipped him around to face the crowd. "Do we believe?" he cried with the tremor again in his voice. The crowd grew hysterical as shouts of "Yes, we believe," echoed from every corner.

Hammond looked at the young man in the wheelchair. He

took the young man's hand in his and said, "Young man, it is time for you to rise up and walk. In God's name I say again, rise, and walk."

The audience was hushed. Some stood quietly. Others dropped to their knees with lips moving silently and tears streaming down their faces. All eyes were focused like arrows toward the young man. He moved. He struggled. He stretched out one leg, then the other. On wobbling legs, he stood slowly to his feet. Hammond held him now by both hands and beckoned to him with a gentle tugging. He took one slow step, and then another. The crowd went wild, cheering and clapping and dancing in the aisles. "Hallelujah! Glory to God!" they shouted.

Trish turned to Kathy with a puzzled, searching expression. But her friend's eyes were riveted on the face of Hammond James. She seemed almost in a trance. By this time, they were all standing, watching the proceedings together. Even Nick was on his feet beside the ladies. Kathy swayed unsteadily and Trish thought for a moment she was going to faint. She reached out and held Kathy securely by the arms and shook her gently. "Kathy," she said softly. Then more firmly, "Kathy, are you okay?" Then her friend moved as if to shake herself awake from deep, delightful sleep.

"Oh, Trish! Did you see that? Isn't he wonderful?" She clasped her hands together tightly and beamed at her friends.

Trish was worried about her. "Let's sit down now, Kathy, until the crowd settles down."

The frenzied crowd was finally quiet once again, and the boy was seated in a regular chair someone had found for him. Hammond held his hands and arms high with his palms facing skyward and spoke again. "Oh, my beloved friends, we have seen a mighty miracle this night." On the word "seen" his voice trembled and was held out like a note of music labeled with a fermata. "God has dwelt among us and has given us so much," he said. The crowd began cheering and clapping again, and Hammond motioned with his hands to quiet them. Then he spoke in his boisterous, clear voice, "What will we give him in return? Look deep into your heart and reach deep down into your pocket. God depends on you, and you, and you," he said, pointing each time he said the word "you" to a different worshiper. His mesmerizing voice rose in volume, pitch and intensity with each pointing of his finger. The offering plates were passed, and the gifts given by the preacher's fans piled high on the plates. Life savings were donated and pledged by some older residents, all in the trembling emotion of the moment. The scene that was played out rivaled the works of Shakespeare himself.

The service was over. The cheers ceased, and the enamored crowd left to return to their individual homes. The trio of friends remained in the background outside the revival tent, and stood together quietly. It was dusk, and the night suddenly seemed to grow cooler. Trish shivered. Perhaps it was the slight chill in the air; perhaps it was a sense of foreboding. Kathy begged her friends to stay with her. She hoped to talk to Hammond.

Kathy was disappointed by the attitude of her friends. Both Trish and Nick were skeptical of the happenings in the service and told her so. "Well," she retorted. "You two just need to believe and trust in what your eyes saw."

Being the investigative reporter that he was, Nick told them, "Let's hang around a while and see what we find out." He left them arm-in-arm in the darkness not far from the great tent, and moved quietly toward the lights he saw still shining inside it. When he was close enough to see inside, his chest heaved with an astonished gasp. He was able to make out the figures of two young boys with Hammond. One was standing, the other was seated in a wheelchair. Their features were identical. Twins. Nick realized with disdain that Hammond had substituted the healthy twin for the crippled one. He shook his head in disgust, and motioned for the ladies to come to him. He put his finger to his lips, signaling them to move quietly. They tiptoed across the parking lot to join him.

Trish and Kathy stood beside Nick and took in the plot of the evening. Kathy's face was pitiful to see. She couldn't help blurting out, "Oh no. This can't be." Her trusting heart ached with disappointment. She thought about how impressed she had been during her times with Hammond and uttered wretchedly, "What a fool I have been." Trish held tightly to her friend.

The preacher turned in their direction. "Who is out there?" his harsh voice called, filled with anxiety. The three friends entered the tent boldly.

"Kathleen, what are you doing here? Who are these people?" He was truly frightened. No one had to speak. Hammond knew that the ruse had been discovered. The mother of the twins began to sob in anguish when she realized these people knew her part in the treachery. She was a kind woman. It was hard and costly to raise twin boys as a single mom. When Hammond offered her the opportunity to make some money to help her make ends meet with this charade, she knew it was wrong, but at least it was a way to provide for them. She covered her face in shame and ran out into the night air. But there was nowhere to go, nowhere to hide her shame. She lingered there in the parking lot, wringing her hands and crying.

"Get out of here!" screamed the furious evangelist.

Nick stood with his fists clenched at his sides. He would have gladly beat the evangelist to a pulp, but the ladies were here. He did have responsibility for them, so he curbed his rage and turned his attention to the young twins. The ladies leaned on each other for comfort, waiting to see what would happen next. Nick spoke to the twins. "Boys, you have no need to be afraid of me. I'm Nick, Nick Danner. Would you mind telling me your names?"

The tall, straight twin finally spoke hesitantly. "I—I'm Tommy, and this is my brother, Bobby," he said as he indicated the boy in the wheelchair. "Thomas and Robert," he stuttered.

Nick smiled reassuringly at Tommy, and they shook hands as gentlemen should. Tommy seemed to relax and let go of some of his nervousness. Nick walked close to Bobby where he sat in the wheelchair. "Bobby, would you mind if I touch your legs? I had an accident similar to yours, and my leg was badly injured, too." Bobby just stared blankly at him, too overwhelmed with the events of the evening to speak.

"It's okay, Bobby," said Tommy to his brother. And Bobby nodded then, giving Nick his permission to touch him. Nick knelt down in front of the crippled boy. His arms reached around the frail body as he placed the right cheek of his head down on the boy's knees. He closed his eyes in intense concentration. A hush fell over the people in the tent. Even Hammond for once kept quiet. Nothing could be heard but the quiet ticking of the small clock that stood on a table near them. It seemed that time and space were suspended. Then once again the words echoed through the tent which had been spoken earlier in a different setting as Nick stood and said, "Take my hand, son, and walk."

A small, almost imperceptible smile came to Bobby's face. Nick noticed that the boy did not laugh or scoff, but he knew that Bobby must surely be thinking, "Well, here we go again." But he placed one hand firmly on one side of the wheelchair and reached his other hand toward Nick, who closed his fingers around the boy's hand and held tightly. Then with a mighty effort, Bobby stood to his feet. Wonder and amazement glowed on his face as he realized the pain he had lived with for so many years due to his broken body had disappeared. He laughed aloud, then took his first step since the night of the accident on Highway 75 when a drunk driver crossed the median and crushed his then strong legs. His twin brother joined his happy laughter as he came to take Nick's place holding the hands of his brother. The joyous laughter was a true delight in the ears of God and man.

"Mom," spoke Bobby. "Where is Mom?" As they listened, they could still hear her broken sobbing from outside the tent. The brothers smiled at each other, one able to know the thoughts of the other without any words, as it had always been with them. "You go, Bobby. You go to Mom," said the unselfish brother.

Haltingly, but growing stronger with each step, Bobby made his way out of the tent toward his anguished mother. "Oh, Tommy, what are we going to do now? Where can we go from here? I just don't think I can make it anymore. How will we pay for Bobby's medical bills?"

"Mom. Mom! Look at me. Please stop crying. It's not Tommy, it's Bobby. It's Bobby, Mom."

Her other strong son walked to them and stood beside his brother. The mother stared. She reached out and held on to her once crippled son's arm. She held it so tightly that it hurt, but Bobby did not mind. She looked deep into her son's eyes and her whole body trembled. Her scream of joy pierced the night. "Bobby, oh Bobby, it is you. You can walk, oh, my dear, dear boy, you can really walk again. Oh, thank God, thank God." And the mother began a hugging and kissing marathon of both her sons.

Nick and his two friends came to join them then. Kathy could not begin to understand what had happened. But Trish knew. She truly believed that somehow the great God that created the universe had given Nick the gift of healing.

Kathy turned back to look only once more at the surly, skulking figure standing in the entrance of the tent. Before she knew the truth, she thought she loved him. Now she hoped never to see him again.

CHAPTER 15

NICK FOUND IT difficult to settle in at his desk at the *Herald* on Monday after what he called the revival fiasco. He wondered as a journalist if he should write about the charlatan Hammond James, or just leave it alone. Nick surmised that this kind of religious circus went on in a lot of places. There were so many horrendous news events these days that a crooked preacher would probably be milk toast to the readers his newspaper could reach.

Nick scratched his head in the back just above his neck, then let his hand fall lower and rubbed his shoulder. Maybe it was a habit. It always seemed to help him think. Maybe he would tell his editor, Mr. D, about the incident at the revival. He would let him make the decision as to whether he should write about James.

Nick could hardly believe what he had experienced himself. He had so many questions. How long had the other twin boy been crippled? The town doctor had verified it in the service. That, at least, was real and not faked. Nick kept asking himself the question over and over, "Why did I feel so compelled to go to the crippled boy and touch him?" It scared Nick; he was still trying to understand the miraculous events that were occurring around him.

He was glad he had found Trish. She was a good listener. She had a caring heart. Though neither of them truly understood the recent strange occurrences, a strong bond was forming between them. They were becoming bound with velvet ropes that could not be easily broken. He longed to be with her now, but he shook his head to clear it and set his mind to the daily tasks ahead. Then without warning, he heard a commotion down the hall. The voices were loud and piercing, some treble and some bass. His eyes grew wider as he took in the scene. Two burly men resembling Saturday night wrestlers were pushing their way through the office, ignoring the calls of "Security, security," from the front desk secretary and a few other employees who joined her.

What a sight in total opposites met Nick's eyes as they barged their way to him. One of the giants held tightly to the left hand of a pixie-faced little girl dressed in a dainty pink dress and black patent leather shoes. The other gargantuan man held her by the right hand. She could have raised her feet and swung between them like a thistle blowing in the wind.

"Nick. It's Nick Danner we are looking for," said a boisterous voice. "Where is he? We heard he was here," said the largest of the two men.

Several Herald employees gathered around the scene. They were silent, but every head turned toward Nick's desk and every eye was focused on him. Nick could not hide. He might as well have been a fallen duck in the weeds being pointed out by a pack of hunting dogs.

"Uh, I'm—I'm Nick Danner," stuttered the astonished young journalist. He gathered enough aplomb to say, "How can I help you, uh, gentlemen?'

Nick was surprised when one of the men slapped him on the back and told him why he had come.

"Mr. Danner, this here is our little sister, Bonnie." He gathered the small girl up into his strong arms and held her as though she were the most precious cargo on earth. "She's a purty little thing, ain't she, Mr. Danner? Smart as a whip, I'm tellin' you, Mr. Danner. But the poor little thing, well, she can't hear none, Mr.

Danner. She was born deaf as a stone post. And we don't want her goin' through life like that, no sir."

"Oh, I'm sorry," said Nick sincerely.

The second brother spoke then. "We heard about what you did up at that revival meeting this weekend, Mr. Danner, healin' that crippled boy and all. You can't keep news like that from spreading as fast as a forest fire." He was silent then, but looked at Nick with great pleading in his eyes. He didn't ask, but Nick knew. He knew what the brothers wanted.

"I—I don't know if I can help."

"Just touch her, Mr. Danner. Please, please, just touch her ears," the smaller brother pleaded.

As the fascinated office staff watched, Nick bent down on one knee before the girl-child. She seemed a little frightened, but knew nothing bad could happen; for she held tightly to the hands of her strong brothers.

Nick raised his hands into the air, his palms facing upward. He gazed at his own hands for a moment. He was awe-stricken at the unearthly drawing of his hands to the little girl. His palms went to her ears and cupped them. He closed his eyes and bowed his head to his chest. To all those looking on, Nick seemed to be praying; but Nick didn't know how to pray. He believed in no deity to whom he could direct his prayers. He only felt the strong, immediate compulsion to hold his hands on her ears.

Nick removed his hands from her ears and stood to his feet. The big men looked down at the little girl they cherished. She laughed her bubbling laugh. They saw her eyes dart from one to the other. She put her hands over her ears and screamed, "Loud! It's so loud. Ouch, it hurts." But she laughed again and the brothers scooped her up and danced her around the room shouting, "Praise God, praise God!"

Cheers went up in the office. Nick's fellow workers were astonished. Mr. D had come into the room and though he didn't understand, he knew that something grand, something newsworthy had happened. It was a delicious scent in his nostrils. It was news.

"Danner! In my office now." Nick nodded like an obedient school boy and followed him.

CHAPTER 16

HAMMOND WAS DISTRESSED that the young news reporter and his friends had caught him in his perpetration of falsehood. He knew he had better clear out of town as fast as he could. All the trappings of his revival were cleared out the next day. It was as if he disappeared into thin air. He was lucky that Nick didn't think he was worth the trouble to investigate. Nick and his friends felt only disgust and distain. They wanted no part of him and his lies.

He planned to stay out of sight of the public for a while to let things cool off in case someone did pick up on the story. He could hardly believe that both the twins were walking that mysterious night. He convinced himself it was just some weird trick of fate, and that the second twin must have somehow been able to walk all along; some psychosomatic illness, or something. He didn't really even care enough to worry about it for very long. What he needed was a new audience. It was time. Hammond was addicted to the spotlight that shone on him at the revival services, and even more addicted to the offerings that poured in when he was preaching in high form. Soon it would be time to get back to work, but he would stay far away from the ones who had found him out.

He had canceled his last three revivals, even though he knew he would lose massive revenue; but the Thomaston revival was still scheduled. He was itching to get back in the pulpit, to be out with the crowd of admirers who for all intents and purposes came to worship him, not the God they claimed to follow.

It felt so good to Hammond James when the Thomaston meetings began. The crowds were eager to let him lead them to the throne of grace each night. And they were willing to pay handsomely for the gift of euphoria that he whipped up with his preaching. He had lost the twins, but at least the blind lady act was intact and it still wowed the crowd.

All in all it had been a successful week of services. Hammond drove back to his hotel in his scarlet-colored convertible with the top down. He felt on top of the world. The rain had even cooperated and held off until the service was finished for the evening. The skies were dark and threatening. Hammond noticed that a warmer than usual wind was blowing across his face as he drove. But still there was no rain.

Hammond parked his car. He felt so high, so good. It was almost like a drug. Not one strong enough to put him to sleep, though. Not like the Atroprophil that he had used on the blonde beauty two months ago. He smiled, a wicked, vile smile that a poisonous viper might have worn if it could smile.

He decided a swim was what he needed to make this a perfect evening. He went to his room, put on his swimsuit, and headed back to the pool. It was quiet and the lifeguard had retired for the evening. The pool lights had been turned off for the night, but Hammond didn't mind. He looked forward to being alone in the cool darkness of the water. It would be a welcome change from the clamor of the revival services.

Hammond prided himself on his diving ability. Maybe it wasn't as good as his preaching, but he found time in his travels to practice at the hotel pools, and he had become quite the diving expert. Too bad no one else was here tonight to see him. He was glad there was no rain yet; just some faint distant rumblings of thunder.

He climbed the ladder to the highest diving board, and was

glad this hotel was classy enough to have one. Nothing but the best for Hammond James. He looked around at the view from the high board. He was glad to be where he belonged, at the top. He laughed aloud in sheer exultation, bounced expertly on the board, and spread his arms for a swan dive, one of his favorites.

His feet left the board and he was airborne with his arms outstretched. Had his revival worshipers been able to see him at this moment, his visage might have brought to their minds the Christ figure to whom they were so devoted.

The quiet night was interrupted at that exact moment by a loud crash of thunder, and a blazing lightning bolt lit up the sky. It seemed to come suddenly out of nowhere. Its bright light lit up the pool, drained of most of its water earlier in the day. And Hammond James was in the spotlight as his body crashed into the gaping jaws of the nearly empty swimming pool.

CHAPTER 17

FOR KATHY, IT was good to be home from college for the summer. She was always a conscientious student, giving her best to her studies. She was fascinated with the study of psychology, probably because she had a gift for loving all kinds of people. She enjoyed her classes, especially those with Dr. Louis. She hadn't been feeling well these past two months, though, and had to put forth great effort to complete her exams in May.

It seemed to her that Dr. Louis was especially attentive to her, and proud of her work in the field of psychology. He was always ready to lend her a helping hand. She closed her eyes and wondered why he was on her mind so much. Kathy dozed. She dreamed of Dr. Louis, but then his face was replaced by the beguiling face of a handsome revival preacher.

This was not the carefree summer that Kathy enjoyed most years. She was restless and listless and wondered if she might be ill. She had stayed bright and happy with her family, not wanting to worry them. But a terrible suspicion nagged at the back of her mind. She was 20 years old now, not a child any more, but a woman of high morals and old-fashioned virtue. What she vaguely suspected, she dismissed as impossible. Yet she knew in the deepest recesses of her mind that she was exhibiting several symptoms of pregnancy.

"Oh, stop being ridiculous," she said out loud to her reflection in her vanity mirror. "Silly girl, it's not the virgin birth again, so stop worrying." Then she knew what she needed to do. After applying fresh lipstick she reached for her purse and car keys and headed for the door.

"Mom, I'm going out on an errand. I will be back soon."

"Okay, Kathy. You won't be long, will you? Dinner is almost ready," asked her mother from the kitchen.

Kathy didn't answer. Her mind was focused on the task at hand. She wondered where to go. She wanted to pick up a pregnancy test, but she certainly didn't want anyone to see her buying it. She decided to drive several miles to a pharmacy that she had not frequented before.

With the test tucked in her purse she headed home. She felt she would soon be rid of this nagging worry.

Kathy ate a few bites, but didn't really taste much of her dinner. She helped her mother to clear the dishes, then headed to her room. She took the little package with her to the bathroom and locked herself in securely for privacy. She giggled nervously at this situation, which seemed so preposterous, and couldn't believe she was here doing this. But she was.

After some minutes that seemed to stretch out interminably, Kathy looked at the test results. She gasped and her free hand flew to her mouth in horror. Her eyes grew wide with disbelief and anguish, and then with fear. She sat for a long time in the lavender bathroom and considered her plight. "God, please help me," she prayed aloud from the innermost part of her being.

The next days were difficult for Kathy. She was anxious and confused. She hadn't been able to bring herself to tell her parents. She longed to talk to Joni, or to Trish, but she was afraid to tell even her best friends. She didn't know what she was going to do. She investigated the unthinkable on her computer when she could get some privacy. Abortion. It would certainly solve the problem at hand. She looked at the pictures of an embryo at four weeks. To her, it didn't really seem like a person yet. Then she saw little fetuses pictured at six weeks, then seven, then eight. She estimated that she was about eight weeks pregnant according to her cycle. She cried when she read that at eight weeks the little being growing inside her could already bend its elbows and its knees. For Kathy, there was only one choice. She knew she could never bring herself to have an abortion.

Kathy's loving mother knew instinctively that something was troubling her daughter. She heard soft sobbing coming from Kathleen's bedroom. She knocked gently on her door.

"Kathy? Kathy darling, may I come in? Please, sweetheart, let me help."

Kathleen wiped her tear-stained face and opened her bedroom door. She fell into her mother's arms, sobbing openly again as if her heart were breaking. "Oh, Mom, Mom," cried the distraught girl. "I don't understand. I don't understand at all."

Kathy and her mother sat together on her bed. Mothers always somehow seem to know the right things to say.

"Kathy," she asked quietly, "Are you in trouble? Are you—are you pregnant, sweet girl?"

"Oh, Mom, yes. Yes, I am. But how can this be? It's impossible. I have been with no man, not that way, Mom. No man that I can remember. I was alone with a man named Hammond James one evening. I don't remember much of what happened that night. But Mom, he is a preacher. He wouldn't…he couldn't have. Trish and I did find that he was doing some deceitful things in his services. He was pretending to heal a blind lady, and a crippled boy. I don't know, I just don't know. I can't remember that evening. I think I embarrassed myself by falling asleep. It's crazy, it's all just crazy."

The mother held her daughter in her arms and let her cry until her tears were exhausted. She didn't speak. She loved and she prayed. Many a tear of her own silently traveled down her face. They would have to face this together.

When her daughter was finally sleeping, her mom pulled a light coverlet over her and tiptoed from her room. She found her husband in the family room watching television. She picked up the remote and turned down the sound. "John, I need to talk with you."

"Can it wait, Mary Ellen? The Aces are behind one run, and there are two men on base."

She clicked the remote and the television screen went black. He scowled at his wife. His face held an annoyed expression, but it soon changed as he read the anguish on his wife's face. John knew immediately that something was truly wrong. "Mary Ellen, what is it? Your face is ashen. Are you sick? Are you hurt?"

She sat beside him on the sofa. She reached out and took both his hands in hers. "John, this is serious. Now stay calm, John, while I tell you something." She gave a huge sigh and plunged ahead. "We think Kathy is pregnant."

"Oh no," declared her husband. "Are you sure? How could this have happened?" Then he answered his own question sarcastically. "Oh, well, the usual way, I guess." He stood up and paced the room. "And who is the father? She certainly must know. Our daughter would never be one to sleep around."

"John, listen to me. Kathy does not know who the father is. She doesn't remember ever being with a man sexually. She can't believe this has happened. She doesn't know how this is possible."

"Perhaps that is what many daughters would tell their shocked parents," John replied. He was feeling hurt about the situation. He idolized his one daughter.

"No, John. I believe her. She said she spent one evening with a preacher whose name is James. Hammond James. She can't remember the two hours she spent with him. They are lost to her."

John stopped pacing. He ran his hand through his still profuse hair and let his open palm rest on the back of his neck. He was an intelligent man with a gift for reading people which he had passed on to his daughter. "Oh, my," he said, dropping his hand to his side. "It sounds like she may have been drugged that night."

"Is that really possible, John? Are there pills that will do that?"

"Yes, Mary Ellen. They are called roofies, and they have been used to take advantage of women for years. Where is this guy? I will kill the rotten scoundrel if he hurt my baby girl."

"I don't know where he is, John. Kathy told me he travels around the state with his revivals. He has been in her college town two years in a row, but she has no idea where he is now."

"We will investigate. I will make a report to the police and ask for help in finding him."

Mary Ellen's thoughts returned to Kathy. "Oh, my poor girl. This is going to be traumatizing for her."

John reached out and held his wife by the shoulders. His strong voice trembled as he spoke. "But we have to find out what happened, don't we, Mary Ellen? Don't we?"

"Yes, John, we do." Then they clung to each other and cried together for the daughter they loved.

CHAPTER 18

KATHY'S MOTHER'S CELL phone sang out from the small desk in her kitchen. She picked it up. "Hello?" she answered. She heard a warm male voice speak to her. "Uh, hello. I was trying to reach Miss Kathy Evans, please."

"May I ask who is calling?" replied Mrs. Evans, politely, but with some curiosity.

"This is Dr. Bruce Louis, Kathy's psychology professor from the University."

"Oh, thank you. Dr. Louis. Just one moment, I will get her to the phone to speak with you."

Mrs. Evans turned to Kathy, her eyes wide with anticipation and questions.

"It's Dr. Louis from the University, Kathy." She motioned with her hand for Kathy to come and take the phone, and gave her a sly smile.

Kathy slowly raised her five months pregnant body from her place on the couch in the den, which was adjacent to the kitchen. She reluctantly took the phone from her mother's hand.

"Hello, Dr. Louis. How kind of you to call," she said. She listened as he spoke to her, very curious herself. After a moment she said, "A new class of Psychology 201 with special field studies?

You want me to be a part of the class?" Her face brightened briefly at the thought of such an interesting prospect. She had forgotten her present situation for just the blink of an eye. She paused, her total senses returning and told him, "I'm very grateful for your call, Dr. Louis. The class sounds wonderful; but I won't be returning to school this semester. I have other, um, pressing matters."

"Oh, I see," said the disappointed voice on the other end of the line. "I am sorry to hear that Kathy. You did such good work last school term. You were an asset to our Psychology Department."

"Thank you, Dr. Louis," spoke Kathy, biting her lip and trying not to cry. "I do wish you the best, though. Goodbye, and thank you again." And he was gone. When she turned to her mother, the dam that held back her tears was broken and she wept in her mother's arms. Her mother was a strong, kind woman. She held her lovingly with no judgment, and let her cry away some of the bitterness and shame she felt. They would get through this together somehow. She remembered the words spoken to her at church, "God will not put more on you than you can bear."

In his office at the university, Dr. Louis was puzzled. He was fond of all of his students. He had the delightful knack of finding something to like in each one of them. But Kathy--she was the prize. He was one of the youngest professors at the university. He had no family other than his students. He shook his head to clear it, and wondered why losing this one student was so devastating to him.

The next several weeks hurried by for Dr. Louis. He worked diligently on his plans for the new semester; in just the last several years he had been teaching, he had already gained the respect of faculty and students. He was ready and eager to meet the new minds that he would be influencing. But there was a shadow lurking just over his shoulder, a nagging anxiousness that he couldn't quite shake.

On the first bright morning of the new semester as he walked across the campus, he heard a voice call out to him. He turned in the direction of the voice and saw that it was Joni Baxter. He recognized her as Kathy's roommate from last year. He had seen them walking together many times on campus, and Kathy had once introduced them hurriedly. He stopped walking and waited for the college co-ed to reach him. She seemed to want to talk with him.

"Hello, Dr. Louis. I am looking forward to being in your Psych 101 class this semester. My friend, Kathy Evans, told me so many good things about you. She made me interested in psychology, too. She really loved your class, Dr. Louis."

The professor felt a quickening in his chest as his heart beat faster at the thought of Kathy. He managed to remain nonchalant, though, as he spoke with Joni. "Thank you. That is always nice to hear. I am always happy to have good new students in my classes, Joni. Uh, but if you don't mind my asking, do you know why Kathy is not returning to school this semester?"

He saw Joni's expression change. They had been walking together as they talked and now they stood alone at a quiet corner of the library building. Joni hesitated, wondering how much to reveal to this kind man. She decided to take the leap. Without even thinking of correct proprieties, she reached out and placed her hand on Dr. Louis's arm as if to steady herself. Or him, she wasn't sure which. "Dr. Louis, Kathy is expecting a baby."

Dr. Louis dropped one of the books he was carrying on the soft grass beneath their feet. He seemed not to notice, but said to Joni, "Oh, I didn't know she had married."

Joni then reached down to retrieve the book he had dropped. She placed it back on the stack with the others he carried and looked straight and deeply into his eyes as she spoke to him earnestly. "Dr. Louis, Kathy didn't marry. She is at home in Atlanta with her parents. She was traumatized to find that she was pregnant. She has been with no one, no man that she can remember. It is a great puzzle."

She paused for Dr. Louis to take it all in. He said in bewilderment, "But how can this be?"

"I don't know, sir," continued Joni. "She does remember visiting one evening with the evangelist, Hammond James. He was here in town last April for spring revival services. But her memory of the night is blank. Her family believes she might have been drugged that night. The police have been called in. Kathy's father has a friend in the sheriff's department and he has been on the case. But they can find absolutely no evidence to continue the investigation. Several months had gone by before Kathy knew she was pregnant, so the trail was cold."

Dr. Louis swore vehemently. His knees suddenly buckled and he slid down the library wall into the soft new-mown grass beneath him, his books falling helter skelter beside him.

Joni kneeled down beside him, noticing that his face had become very pale. "Dr. Louis, are you ok? Shall I call for someone to help?"

"No, Joni. I will be all right in a moment. It's just that, that—I sent her to him. She asked me if she could go and interview him for a class project. I never dreamed, I never thought...do they really think this is what happened, Joni?"

"We just don't know, Dr. Louis. Kathy is such a fine girl, with high morals and standards. The dormitory girls teased her and called her 'Miss Goody Two Shoes.' But I think some of them secretly admired her strong stance on the sanctity of marriage. I knew her better than anyone on campus, I guess, and I don't believe this could have ever happened to Kathy without some foul play somewhere."

"Will you talk with me again, Joni?" asked Dr. Louis as he picked up each of his books and once more stacked them neatly in his arms. "I really must be getting to my class. I'm afraid I am late already."

"Of course, Dr. Louis. I will talk with you any time," Joni assured him. "We both care about her, don't we, sir?"

"Yes, Joni. Absolutely," the professor replied.

Joni watched the tall, handsome figure as he hurried away, still wearing an intense frown of concern on his face. Though she realized she had made him sad and confused, she did not regret telling him about Kathy. Deep in her spirit, she felt it was exactly the right thing to do.

CHAPTER 19

MARTY CULVER STOOD across the street from the magnificent Calcine Hotel on Ansley Street. He had studied the pictures of the Winecoff Hotel which stood on this same parcel of land until it caught fire on December 7, 1946. All of its 13 floors had succumbed to the mammoth appetite of the flames, which took the lives of 119 people. Marty knew it remained the deadliest hotel fire in U.S. history. His eyes climbed the height of the building, resting on each floor for a moment. It seemed to mock him, taunting him silently, but with vehemence, "See, we can come back. We are here again."

Marty impatiently changed his weight from one foot to the other, willing to stand for hours to look at this architectural marvel. To gaze at the structure was to him like eating fresh honey from a hollow in a mighty tree; a treasure, a delight, as drawing for him as the siren song had been to Ulysses. He was barely conscious of the swishing rhythm of the cars as they passed by one by one. He didn't care who was in the cars going by. Those human strangers meant nothing to him. He didn't really think much of the human race. He liked buildings better. He had always liked to try to draw them. When he realized his drawings were improving each year, he wondered if he might someday have the chance to be an architect.

Fat chance. His mother could hardly keep them financially afloat doing what menial jobs she could.

Buildings had a form and a beauty that was irresistible to Marty; in his twisted mind, this fascination was not very far afield from the beauty he saw in a young girl being held captive by a serial killer. The beauty was delicious, but only if there was power to destroy it. That was real power--to hold the loveliness in the palm of your hand; to have the choice, to keep it in your vision, or to destroy it. According to this bewildered and confused young man, having that choice was his power. And he wanted power. He had to have power, for someone in his past had always had power over him. The automobiles sped by in a colorful pattern and Marty's mind traveled to his past.

The memories lived in a special box deep in Marty's brain. He tried hard not to open it too often. The abuse had sickened him from his earliest days as a little boy. The burly, unshaven, heavy-set man came into his room at night. The odor of alcohol had seared Marty's nostrils. "Ready for our games, Marty?" the giant man would ask him with his slurred voice.

"No!" his silent voice cried inside, but no answers were spoken out loud for the night to hear. Where was his mother? He always wondered. Sometimes he had seen her shaking and crying in the small kitchen where she seemed to always be busy on early evenings, but she never seemed to be available to him later in the evening when the giant man came. Perhaps she was serving ham and eggs or hamburgers at the dingy restaurant where she worked as a waitress. Marty wished that he had a father to help him. He could not remember a time when there had been a daddy in his life, only his mother and the giant.

Marty shut the box in his mind. Ah, what a wonderful building it is, thought Marty as he gazed across the street at the tall building reaching toward the sky. The windows were like mirrors, causing him to squint and put his hand to his forehead above his eyebrow to ward off the sharp shards of the sunlight. His lip curled softly at one corner as his mind worked on the plan; it had started with a seed that surprised him at the beginning, even making him laugh at the absurdity of it. But the seed grew in the foul soil of sorrow and abuse; and its roots grew deeper until it had a strong foothold deep in Marty's psyche.

CHAPTER 20

IT WAS FINALLY the end of the school day. Marty cautiously stowed away in the high school auditorium. It was one of the few days he was counted present at school. His attendance was sporadic and the principal was starting to get involved. But on this particular day, he sat through every class, watching the clock, waiting for it to give the signal that school was over for the day.

When most of the students and faculty had cleared the school building, Marty crept from his hiding place. He made his way to the drama department's costume closet. He had shrewdly consulted the internet for the uniforms worn at the Celine Hotel. He wanted to blend in and not call attention to himself. He laughed quietly as he came upon the clothes he needed. "Yes, you are just what I need," he said to the black pants, white shirt and grey vest that he took from the closet. The clothes were mute, offering no thanks for the compliment they had been given.

Marty entered the hotel through a side door. The security guard was busy talking and pointing to a map showing Atlanta sights to a group of visitors on tour. Marty was relieved to discover that he had gone unnoticed as he completed the first step of his plan.

He walked with a nonchalant gait to his destination—the

hotel laundry room. He found the space he needed was deserted, the charm of lucky circumstance once again with him. "Hurry, hurry, while you have the chance," Marty's inner voice whispered to him. He closed the door behind him and paused to take several deep breaths as he listened to the bumpy, percussive song of the dryers. He found a hamper heavily loaded with hotel linens and used it to block the entrance door.

He kneeled down and took the milk carton of kerosene from his carefully arranged pack. The two books of matches he had brought were sleeping soundly in his pocket, awaiting their chance to come alive. His hands retrieved the row of firecrackers that were securely tucked into the bottom of his treasured package. He would not set them off, for that would make too much noise. He tore open the first firecracker, and then another and a third as well. The firecrackers gave up the grey powder that was inside. Marty scattered the powder on the laundry room floor. Then he took the carton of kerosene and with careful steps made swirls in the grey powder that were strangely similar to the swirls in the 'Starry, Starry Night' painting of Vincent Van Gogh.

Marty had no thought now for himself, or the hotel inhabitants. He had only his goal, only his purpose. His single desire was to satisfy his compulsive need for vengeance for the pain that lived deep in his subconscious.

He took a book of matches from his pocket. The red phosphorus of the match tips called to him. He struck a match against the powdered glass of the strip that adorned the book of matches for just such a purpose. A small ripple of laughter escaped again from the young arsonist. His eyes opened wide as he saw the match burning brightly. Marty dropped it into the kerosene swirls. Quickly, he repeated the process, taking a step away from the first flames he had caused to bloom. He relished the scene, for this was his moment in time.

"Get out of here, now, Marty," cried the inner voice again to him. "Hurry!"

Marty went toward the hamper to move it. He had intended to leave the room sooner, but he was transfixed by the brilliant beauty of the fire for a moment too long. As Marty pulled the hamper away from the door, a blue and yellow flame licked at his pants leg. In his rapt attention to his venomous task, he had failed to notice the tiny rivulets of kerosene that had dripped from the plastic carton onto his clothes. The flame traveled upward to his shirt and grey vest. Marty cried out in anguish. He barely heard the fire alarms in the streets as the bright red vehicles raced to the scene. He writhed in pain. He dropped to the floor, but that was no help, for it was flooded with flame. Attendants burst into the room, as their fire extinguishers spewed their encapsulated contents. And Marty screamed.

CHAPTER 21

PEOPLE HAD BEGUN to talk about Nick. Rumors and stories passed from one person to another. Were the incidents they were hearing about just coincidence? The brothers had spread the news of their little sister being able to hear for the first time. Many had seen firsthand Nick's involvement at the stadium with the injured player. Mr. D had asked Nick about these mysterious events; he was not quite sure in his mind how to catalog them yet. He kept his focus on printing real and truthful facts in his *Atlanta Herald*, and he had no proof of these amazing events. He tried to keep the events under wraps as much as possible. When some of Nick's closest fellow employees asked about the incidents, he just shrugged his shoulders and kept his silence.

On this particular bright morning, it was called to Mr. D's attention that a crowd was gathering in front of the newspaper building. "You had better come see this, Mr. D," coaxed one of his faithful writers. It was hard to resist her pleas.

He begrudgingly got up from his desk. He was involved in work that needed to be done; but he followed her to the front of the building and looked out a front window. He was surprised at what he saw; for there on the news building steps, a chattering group of people of various heights, ages and ethnicities had collected. The many hues of their colored coats sparkled in the sunlight like an artist's palette. "What in the world?" he asked, as his eyes took in some visitors on crutches and several in wheelchairs.

Mr. D turned to his staff member, raised his eyebrows, and threw his hands out palms up at his sides questioningly.

"They are asking for Nick, Mr. D." The lovely girl paused, weighing her next words carefully for a moment. "They believe he can heal them," she explained.

"Good grief," snorted Mr. D. "I'm going back to work in my office. Find Nick Danner and send him to me as soon as you can, will you?"

"Will do, Mr. D," said Sheila respectfully. She liked her gruff boss and wished to please him.

Nick was summoned and went speedily to knock on Mr. D's office door. "Well, don't just stand out there, Nick. Come in here and help me figure out what is going on in front of the building."

"I saw the crowd, Mr. D. Should I go out to them? They do seem to be calling for me."

They heard Mr. D's phone ring insistently then, begging him to answer. He heard other phones ringing at the reporters' stations as well. He picked up the phone and before he could even answer he heard someone shout into his ear, "Fire. A fire on Ansley Street."

"Fire?" he asked incredulously. "Fire at the Celine Hotel on Ansley? Yes, we will get someone there immediately."

As he hung up he heard the sirens begin to scream in the city streets. Nick was hanging on to Mr. D's every word, his adrenaline pumping and his fists clenched as he awaited instructions. "Nick boy," bellowed Mr. D. "Fire at the Celine Hotel on Ansley. Get there as soon as you can."

Nick nodded and turned to leave, but then he remembered what they had seen in front of the building. "The crowd on the front sidewalk?" questioned Nick. "I don't know if I can get through."

"Go out the back way and take my car. It's out back. You saw it when I bragged on it last month. But don't damage it. I've only made one payment on it and my wife will kill me if anything happens to it." He picked up his keys and tossed them to Nick.

The young reporter exited his boss's office and headed toward the back entrance in record time. He went by his desk on his way out, and it suddenly occurred to him that it was cold outside. As he raced toward the back door of the building, he grabbed his jacket from where it was casually draped on the back of his desk chair. He loved that jacket. He had about worn it out these past few years, wearing it to keep out the raw and sometimes biting Georgia wind.

Once in the car, Nick heard the sirens as he sped toward the Celine Hotel. Luckily, most of the traffic lights in his path glowed green as he traveled toward the endangered hotel. He arrived and parked his car illegally, knowing from past experience that his press pass would rule out any penalties. In a crisis such as this, illegally parked vehicles would be the fire department's least concern.

Nick's eyes grew wide and his heart raced as he walked as close as he dared to the scene of the fire. The brave firemen had given the job their best effort. Though a great deal of smoke billowed from the lower floors, the flames were being brought under control. This would not be a repeat of the 1946 event that claimed 119 lives on the same spot when the Winecoff Hotel was demolished by a monster fire. Nick would not have the chance that the young reporter had years ago when he snapped the picture of a girl in mid-air who had jumped from one of the high floors in the Winecoff Hotel to avoid the flames. During that long-ago fire, that particular camera man had won the Pulitzer Prize. But Nick would have preferred that the circumstances be different this time if he could choose. His heart was pure.

Nick's camera was aimed and was digesting the scene. Through the lens of his camera, he saw ambulances parked in front of the hotel. Nick's camera gave its percussive click as he watched an ambulance driver and a fireman bring a body out of the building on a stretcher. The driver opened the back doors of the ambulance. Nick wondered if the occupant of their appointed stretcher was still alive.

In the turmoil, Nick was surprised to recognize the ambulance driver. He was a good friend from years past by the name of Matt Bolton. Their eyes met for a brief moment. Matt nodded to Nick and his lips curved in the slightest of smiles, but this was not a time for reconnections.

Nick stood by as the victim of the fire was put into the ambulance. He stilled his camera for the time being. The fireman spoke over the noise to Matt, "I have to get back to making sure the fire is stopped. Can you take it from here?"

"I will get him to Emergency right away," he assured the fireman. But he looked around with a worried frown on his face. He again spotted Nick standing by like a soldier on guard. "Hey, Nick. What a day it has been. My assistants have all been called to other emergencies. I hate to leave this patient by himself, but I have to drive the ambulance. Any chance you could get in and ride to the hospital with him?"

Nick did not hesitate. "Of course, Matt, I'll be glad to do that."

Nick climbed into the back of the ambulance, the doors closed, and he found himself alone with the badly burned victim. His heart went out to him. His hair was badly singed on one side. Nick could not stop himself. Wanting him to know that someone cared, he reached out to gently stroke the part of the boy's head that had escaped the licking flames of the fire. Although he was badly burned, the boy was indeed alive. But Nick knew he was clinging to life, and could not possibly live much longer. Nick heard the barest whisper of Marty's voice: "Cold. So cold." Nick longed to comfort him. He remembered his warm jacket, and took it off hurriedly and wrapped it over and around the flame-ravaged body of young Marty.

The ambulance sped through the city streets and they quickly reached the emergency entrance to the hospital. His friend, Matt, opened the rear doors. Nick jumped from the ambulance to make room for the hospital attendants who swiftly and deftly carried Marty into the hospital.

Nick stood quietly and watched, hoping for the best. There was no time to retrieve his beloved, old jacket. It still covered the burn victim as he was rolled down the hall, and its zipper reflected the bright lights of the emergency room.

Matt shook Nick's hand warmly. "So good to see you, buddy, and thanks for the help. Sorry to run, but they have called me to another location. Let's get together when we can. Okay?" And he was gone.

Nick stood in the parking lot contemplating his next move. He decided the right thing to do would be to contact Mr. D and let him know the situation.

"Just stay there for a while, Nick," his boss instructed. "This may end up being a big story. I realized after you left that the Celine Hotel is on the same spot as the Winecoff fire of 1946. My nose for news is twitching and something is telling me the two fires may be connected."

"Okay, sir. I will stay here for a while and see what I can find out."

Nick went to the waiting area and settled in a green, sterile chair. His mind went to the events that had just happened. They played in his mind like a video that kept rewinding. He had no knowledge of the young man who was burned, but he pitied him. He wondered if he had, indeed, been the one who started the fire. He was anxious to know more details. He waited patiently, but as he was not a relative, no one came to bring him news about Marty.

The clocked ticked and minutes turned to hours. Nick drank a cup of coffee from the vending machine and waited. When two hours had passed he went to the receptionist desk and identified himself. He politely asked if he could have information on the burn case that had recently come in.

The receptionist was a bit skeptical, but in view of his press credentials, she told him she would try to find someone to speak with him if he would wait in the waiting area.

Nick went back to the place to which he had been relegated and waited once more. Another hour was gone, and when he thought he might just leave for now, the double doors opened and an attractive doctor in blue came through them and called out, "Mr. Danner?"

"Yes. Here," responded Nick, so glad to hear his name called.

She ushered him to a quiet private area and introduced him to a stately matron waiting there to join them. "Mr. Danner, this is Mrs. Braxton, one of our hospital administrators."

The correct polite greetings ensued and the three of them were soon seated together. "Mr. Danner, you are from the *Atlanta Herald*, I believe? Please tell us how we can help you."

"I was at the Celine Hotel where there was a fire today. I rode back in the ambulance with a badly burned young man at the request of my friend, Matt Bolton. I am interested in the condition of the patient."

No one spoke for what seemed to Nick an interminably long moment. He glanced at the doctor. Her lips seemed to be purposely locked firmly together. The doctor looked toward the administrator, who began to speak, choosing her words very carefully.

"Mr. Danner, if I may be perfectly candid with you, this has been a strange case for us. The patient you are inquiring about was brought into emergency here. His first attendants and the emergency doctor who was on duty at the time brought him to the burn unit. However, they must have made a mistake."

The doctor blurted out, "But Administrator Braxton, I saw him myself. He was..."

"That will be all, Doctor Johnson. You may go now, and please see me later when your rounds are finished," directed the strong voice of the administrator.

She left them alone, and some of the light seemed to vanish from the room.

"Where is he," Nick asked Mrs. Braxton. "Where is the patient now? Will he recover?"

"I must tell you, Mr. Danner, that the young man is no longer a patient with us."

"Oh, he didn't make it then. I'm sorry to hear that."

"Oh, no, he did not die, Mr. Danner. He has been taken away by the police authorities to be questioned as a possible arson suspect."

"But—but how is that possible? He wasn't well enough."

The administrator's head fell to her chest and she took a deep breath, closing her eyes for a moment. She was not an unkind soul, but she had to do what was required of her to protect the hospital she worked for. She seemed to be gathering the strength she would need to bring this young reporter to her side.

When she spoke it was with great firmness. "You see, Mr. Danner, that's the thing about it. There must have been some kind of mix up when he came in. For some reason, he was transported to our burn unit. But when he was examined there, the doctor found no burns on his body. Nada." Her hands forcefully crossed each other in front of her body, stating silently and eloquently the sign for the word she spoke, "Nothing."

"I don't understand," stammered Nick.

"Neither do we, Mr. Danner." Her voluminous brown eyes had a pleading expression as she looked directly at him. "I have been instructed to ask you to please keep this part of the fire story under wraps, so to speak. We want our patients to feel secure about our records and standards of procedure here. We feel that if news of our mistaken diagnosis was allowed to reach the public, it could be a detriment of some proportion to us. Can we count on you, Mr. Danner? Will you consider our wishes on this matter?"

Once again, Nick did not hesitate. He knew that even if there was a momentous story for his newspaper here, he would not pursue it unless ordered to. It could do too much damage to the hospital. He would follow up with the police authorities about the alleged arsonist.

"Yes, of course," Nick replied, and he saw the enormous mixture of relief and hope on the administrator's face. She stood, smiled and offered her hand to Nick. He took her hand and held it for a moment in a farewell gesture. She turned to go, but then stopped abruptly and turned back to him once more. She reached behind the chair she was sitting in.

"Oh I almost forgot, Mr. Danner, this nice jacket was left here during the time when all this happened. It was draped over the patient when he came in, but he later told us it wasn't his. He did remember having it placed over him while he was in the ambulance. He said when the kind stranger gave it to him he felt much warmer and it seemed to relieve his pain. Would this jacket happen to be yours, Mr. Danner?"

CHAPTER 22

THE STUDENTS IN Dr. Louis's class had noticed that he seemed distracted and worried lately. He was a favorite among the university faculty because of his kind nature and willingness to assist each young person in his classes. They knew he was writing a book. He had shared that with them. It would be a great coup for him to be the published author of *Psychology for Building a Better Tomorrow*. They decided perhaps this was what was pressing on his mind.

Dr. Louis had more on his mind than the book he was writing. He could not stop thinking of Kathy Evans. She was gone, and he knew that his students would come and they would go. But she seemed to be ever on his mind, and she haunted his dreams.

Seated in his office one September afternoon, he paused and took his fingers from the keyboard. He decided his manuscript could wait. It was time. It was time to be decisive. He found Kathy's telephone number and dialed it.

"Hello," answered the sweet voice he remembered so well.

"Uh, Kathy, hello. Bruce Louis here. How are you? We miss you on campus." He searched for the right words to say.

Kathy spoke into the receiver after a surprised pause. "Oh, hello, Dr. Louis. How nice of you to call."

His heart began to race and his pulse quickened as he heard her voice, which to him was angelic.

"Um, Kathy, I was wondering--would it be possible for you to look over the book project I am pursuing? Your written papers for me were always outstanding. I could really use your help; another pair of eyes on the manuscript, you know."

Kathy was both astounded and delighted at his words. "Why, yes, I would be honored, Dr. Louis. Will you send me a copy of your pages?"

"I would really like to do this work in person with you, Kathy. Would that be possible? I would be glad to come to your home in Atlanta, on the weekend, if that would be convenient for you."

As he waited for her response, he wondered if he had gone too far. But after a pause of a few seconds that seemed like minutes to him, she gave him the answer he had hoped for. "Why, yes, Dr. Louis. My family and I would be happy to have you visit in our home."

Their times together grew more and more frequent. As he had always suspected, it was as if they were meant for each other. When they first began to meet, he let her know wisely and gently that he knew about her coming child. He offered no condemnation, only understanding and love. For he realized that he did love her; he was as certain of that as he was that the sun would rise each day in the east.

On one special visit to her home in Atlanta, he carried a special small black box in his pocket. As they shared a quiet moment looking at the now almost completed manuscript, Dr. Louis set the pages aside and took her hands in his. "Kathy, my sweet Kathy, I love you so. Will you marry me?" The box appeared from his pocket, a shining diamond ring nestled in its silken lining.

"Oh, yes, Bruce," she cried as she flung her arms around him with incredible joy. When she finally released him from the embrace, he took the ring and placed it on the fourth finger of her trembling left hand. And once again they rejoiced in each other's arms.

CHAPTER 23

TONY GIOVANELLI HELD his sobbing wife in his arms. He could do nothing to console her; nothing but hold her in the circle of his arms. Those arms were strong and muscular and his six foot, two inch frame dwarfed the lovely raven-haired lady with the sad eyes. The wealthy leader of the Giovanelli mob had also shed bitter, angry tears. He tried hard to keep his weeping for his little son out of sight of his beloved Maria.

"How can this be?" she cried aloud between her sobbing as her chest heaved and lurched and she felt she would stop breathing. "Our little caro bambino, our only son, so sick, so sick. I can't bear it, I can't, I can't. Oh Tony, do something, do something. You are so powerful—so many people follow you. So much money, so many grand things you have provided for us. And now we can do nothing for our son?"

He held her gently as he told her again as he had many times, "My Maria, you know that we have had the very best doctors available. They have tried. I offered everything, I would give up everything, to save our little one. At least we had two precious years with him. We saw Marco take his first steps, we heard him say Mama and Papa. We saw him so happy before he fell ill. We must be thankful for the time we had with him."

"Oh, no, no," screamed Maria, her heart aching. "Not enough time, not enough! And you know we cannot have another child. I am not able. Our only son. Your namesake." Her eyes grew wide with anguish as another thought came to her. "You will leave me. I will lose you and little Marco." She broke down once more into pitiful, wretched sobs.

"Never, my sweet Maria," said Tony, as he placed soft, tender kisses on her forehead and her cheeks, kissing away the salty tears. They cried together then, holding each other until they were exhausted and could cry no more. Still holding each other close, they walked together to the nursery where their two-year-old son's faithful nurse was closely watching over him. It was hard to gaze on his small body, so weakened from the rare and incurable virus. He had once been so vibrant and healthy. The doctor had told them to say their goodbyes, for the time was growing short.

Nurse Anna said to the distraught couple, "You both should get some rest, dear friends. Go and lay down for a while. You know I will keep watch as though he were my own. You both must keep your health and strength for the days ahead. God will help you."

"God has forsaken us, Anna," spoke Maria bitterly. The stillness in the nursery room was almost unbearable.

Their rapt attention was suddenly broken by an urgent and loud banging at the front door. "Tony," called the voice of his younger brother, "Tony, let us in." Tony turned away from his son and walked slowly to the door. He didn't have the strength to hurry, and walked as if he was in a fog. He reached the door and opened it for Joey. His younger brother took him squarely by the shoulders and looked earnestly into his face. When he realized Tony was almost sleep-walking, he shook him gently. "Tony, Tony, listen to me. I have something important to tell you."

Rousing from his stupor, Tony mustered enough strength to give his attention to what his brother was saying, "Yes, Joey, what is it?"

"I wanted to tell you, I heard of a man; a man who heals the sick. He has gone into hiding, into reclusion, because he could not handle the crowds of people who were hounding him. No one knows where he is, but could we find him, Tony? With your connections, could we possibly send out some of your best men to find him, and bring him back to little Marco? At least it would be a chance."

The words of Tony's brother were like a shot of adrenalin in his tired veins. He came alive at once and said, "Call the families together. Everyone who can help. Friends. Enemies. I will make it all right. We will scour the world for this man who could possibly help my son. We must find him!"

CHAPTER 24

NICK SAT AT the kitchen table in the small north Georgia cabin that had been his home for a few months now, at the suggestion and generosity of Mr. D, who had promised to keep his job open for him. Lonely as he was, he feared going back to the busy unintended celebrity that had drained all his energy. He was even afraid for his life, so many people were clawing their way to him because of the gift that had come upon him. He didn't understand. He just knew that he had to stay in hiding as long as his money held out. Then what? A new identity? A new country?

"It isn't fair. I didn't ask for this," he cried aloud into the mountain air. He knew he had helped so many people, and he was glad. But not satisfied. He longed to see Trish, but to keep her safe, he felt it was best not to even let her know where he was.

Nick's lonely reverie was suddenly disturbed by lights outside, the headlights of a long, black car. He knocked over his kitchen chair as he jumped up from the table, startled and wary. "Oh, no," he said aloud as he saw the black-clothed figures climb from the car, carrying guns.

Suddenly the door burst open and several burly men entered the small cabin. He gasped as he saw each one had drawn a gun.

It was like a dream sequence that couldn't possibly be really happening to him.

"Are you Nicholas Danner?" asked the gunman in front.

"Y—yes," stuttered Nick, barely able to answer the fierce looking man. He was slightly aware of a cold sweat that trickled down his back from his neck. His hands were clammy. He was hoping he would not soil his pants. He was afraid, more afraid that he had ever been in his life.

The gunman spoke again, "We were sent here by Tony Giovanelli. He needs your help. His young son is dying. We were instructed to find you and bring you to him. We hope you will come peacefully; if not, we will encourage you in whatever way necessary. You have no choice. You must come with us. No need to gather your belongings. You will receive all you need." Then as an afterthought, the forceful stranger said, "Please." But he did not smile.

Nick knew it was senseless to resist. He only had one option: to go with them. He soon found himself in the back seat of the dark limo, and though it was comfortable, he did not stop shaking for quite a while. The miles sped past and he even slept for a bit after he calmed down.

He was awakened by iron gates swinging open for the limo to pass through. They began winding up a long drive until a massive, elegant mansion came into view. It appeared to him to be a castle. He gazed in awe and wondered what it must be like to live such a lifestyle as this.

They drove to the front doors and stopped, and someone opened the car door for Nick. As he stepped out, he saw the most beautiful Italian woman he had ever seen standing on the porch landing. She was clinging to a tall, prince of a man. His escorts led him up the steps to the waiting parents.

Tony reached out quickly for Nick's hand, almost dragging him forward. "Oh, thank you for coming. This is my wife, Maria.

We are in desperate need of your help. We have heard that you, that you..." His voice choked and he could not go on.

"Sometimes I can help, Mr. Giovanelli. I will certainly give it my best efforts. I can only say perhaps. Can you show me the child?"

"Please, come this way," said Maria, leading Nick to the boy's nursery upstairs. Her husband followed them as the others waited below. The guns were no longer visible. Burley men seated around the massive gathering room prayed silently if they knew how. Some hoped and wished all good things to come to pass. Tony's son was loved by many, as all little children are beloved by humanity. They are life. They are the future.

Nick's heart was wrenched as he looked at the small form of the boy child, so pitiful and silent in the crib. The mask of death was upon him. Nick closed his eyes, wanting to transport himself away from the scene of impending death. He reflected on his time in solitude at the cabin. It had been so good. There he found the rest he needed so badly. He had been so weary of giving so much of himself. He didn't want to heal anymore. He didn't understand why the universe had dropped this dauntless task onto his lap. Too much. Too hard. But he opened his eyes once again and looked at the little boy, and tears filled his eyes until they ran over and down his face. He reached for the small, withered body and drew the sick child into his arms. He sat down in the rocking chair in the nursery, held him to his chest and rocked him ever so gently for a few moments as the mother and father held hands and wept quietly. No one spoke. There was no movement other than the gentle rocking of the healer and the child. Then Nick placed the boy back into the crib and said softly, "We shall see what we shall see."

They watched the sleeping child intently. He seemed so still, he made no sound or movement, yet now he seemed so exquisitely peaceful. As many a mother has done before, Maria leaned over to touch the still form, to check his breathing. Tony heard his wife gasp and reached out for her. She swayed in his arms, then regained her composure and cried out with joy.

"His eyes, he opened his eyes!" Within a few moments Marco began to move and stretch his arms and legs. He reached his arms up for his mother to lift him out of the crib.

Tony moaned with an incredible sound, born of anxiety and desperation that had instantly turned to joy. "Bambino, oh, my precious son. You are better, you will live."

And Nick Danner reeled in the intoxication of the incredible elixir from the vine of healing that apparently stretched invisibly to heaven. Though he did not understand, it was an experience that could be matched by no other. He knew it was time to return to his life. The gift he had been given was not his to hide. It was his to share, and he had no choice but to open his life to the hurt, the suffering, and the wounded, to help them any way he could. For whatever reason it happened, it was his destiny, and he knew that now. Perhaps things would become clearer in time.

CHAPTER 25

NICK HAD FOUND new strength and a new perspective on what was happening in his life, although he still felt in the dark about so many things. He made his way back to Atlanta from his mountain retreat. To her delight and relief, he contacted Trish immediately upon his return. She talked him into meeting her at the fountain in front of her school. She led Nick to a bench and they sat down together. They were alone. "Oh, Trish, what is happening to me? I don't understand why this has happened, and I certainly don't have a clue as to how to handle it." He bent his head and covered his face with his palms. No words that seemed suitable came to her. It was a relief that no one was around. She sat at Nick's side, holding his hand. She let him weep unashamedly, and she wiped tears from her face as well. She wanted so much to help him. She was amazed at what had been happening in his life, for she cared for him deeply and it affected her life as well. They were both frightened. She held tightly to Nick's hand, waiting for his calmness to return.

"Dear, sweet Nick, something has come alive in you and given you a special power. Was it you, Nick, was it really you that helped Joe Turner? And the little deaf girl? What about the fire, Nick? What really happened in the fire?"

Nick shook his head from side to side as he answered her with great wonder evident in his voice. "I wish I had an answer for you, Trish. I am as puzzled and bewildered as you are."

They sat together silently. A cool breeze blew across their faces and brought some refreshment. Looking for a way to ease the tension, Trish called his attention to a bug that had landed on her hand. It gave them a new focus. Grateful for any distraction, Nick said to her, "That insect is a June bug, Trish. When I was a boy we used to catch one and tie a thread around its leg, and the bug would fly round and round our heads in a circle. I guess it was kind of cruel if you think about it. Maybe we should have just watched it and let it fly its own way."

"I guess that is how God is with human beings," said Trish. "He could make us do what he wants us to do, but He leaves us free to choose our own way." The little insect spread its wings and they watched it fly away.

"Makes me think of my Great-Granny June, Nick. She was always telling us grandkids, "He prayeth best who loveth best all things both great and small; for the dear Lord who madeth them, he made and loveth all."

"I know that one, Trish. That's Samuel Taylor Coleridge from *Rhyme of the Ancient Mariner.*"

"That's right," said Trish, nodding her head.

"Did you say 'Great-Granny June,' Trish?" commented Nick, the color beginning to return to his handsome face. "She must be as old as dirt." He smiled, teasing her.

"Nick, shame on you. What an expression." She smiled at him to let him know she wasn't really angry. "Yes, Great-Granny June is getting up there. She was 91 on her last birthday. But her mind is still clear as a bell and she has all her faculties. I think she is the wisest and most spiritual person I know."

"You seem pretty wise yourself, Trish; wise beyond your years, so the saying goes."

"But not like her, Nick. It's like she has a connection beyond this world we live in. She seems to know everything. We all got in terrible trouble when we were small if someone whispered that she might be, you know, strange. She always seemed like an angel to me. Something heavenly, something—" Trish stopped mid-sentence. Her face lit up. "Nick, maybe she could help us figure out more about what is going on," she said. She grabbed his hand and squeezed it. He could not help being affected by her contagious excitement.

"Tell us what, Trish?"

"Why, tell us what is happening with you, Nick. Tell us why this mysterious gift has come to you."

Nick nodded his head affirmatively as he said with no reservations, "That is one puzzle I would really like to have solved, Trish."

"Let's go to see her, Nick. She isn't far from here. She lives at the Haven Assisted Living Home in Kennesaw. She is happy and busy there. Even at her age, she practically runs the place, I hear. Everyone loves Great-Granny June."

Trish stood and clapped her hands together like a little girl. Nick thought she grew more charming with every bit of time he spent with her. She was getting under his skin, but in a very nice way. The pair walked away together with new purpose, Trish still chattering excitedly like the birds on an early spring morning.

CHAPTER 26

TRISH AND NICK were greeted at the well-known assisted living center by the attractive and polished Barbara Livingston. It was to her credit that the reputation of this facility was immaculate and promising to all residents, and welcoming to visitors. She recognized Trish immediately, and after the proper introduction to Nick, she said, "I will be happy to bring Great- Granny June to you."

Great-Granny June was delighted to hear that her great-granddaughter was coming to visit, and bringing a young man, too. She was extremely pleased when Trish called and asked if they could come. They would arrive at two o'clock. She put on her prettiest blue frock and vanilla Sunday-best shawl. Josephina, her assigned helper at Haven, walked with her to the main parlor where visitation was held. She made her as comfortable as possible in a soft chair, for Great- Granny June had a bowed and crooked back that caused her to have to walk bent over almost double. Her face almost pointed to the floor as she walked. But what a face it was—a unique oval, a mass of smile wrinkles surrounded by snow white hair with a tiny nose. Her face looked as though it could easily fit into the space of a small skillet; or as one thoughtless young man had once said to her, "You look like your face got smashed in by a truck." The tiny face was always gilded with a radiant smile.

She beamed at her great granddaughter when she saw her come through the door. She raised her face proudly as high as she could and waved her hand in greeting to Trish and her young man. "Come here to Granny June, you sweet girl," exclaimed Great-Granny June.

Trish came to her, knelt down and put her arms around her. "Hello, my darling Great-Granny June. How are you?"

Nick was standing behind her. He was ill-prepared for the sight of this poor old fairy-like creature that was so loved by Trish. She had failed to tell him how crippled she was, probably because she saw her only through the eyes of love.

Nick managed to conceal his surprise and greeted the matriarch warmly. "So glad to meet you," he said as he took her wizened hand in his and held it for a moment.

Nick thoughtfully moved two chairs up close to the place where Great-Granny June was seated and they chatted happily. "I'm glad you are here, child," said the loving elder. "But, I know you, little Patricia, I can tell you have something on your mind. Something is troubling you. Is there any way I can help you? The two of you?" She was always quick to include every soul within her hearing. "When you share your troubles with others, the burden always becomes lighter."

"Oh, Great-Granny June, you know me so well," declared Trish, her eyes intent on her great grandmother's face. "We do need your help." Trish looked at Nick, then turned back to the one who had loved her so long. She said, "I don't know where to begin."

"Well, child, the best place is always the beginning."

Trish nodded her head in agreement. "I have to warn you, though, our story is unusual and hard to believe."

"I'm listening," Great-Granny June assured the girl.

"It's about Nick. Something incredible, even miraculous, has happened to Nick. He—he has somehow gained the power to heal. He touches people and their sickness, their infirmities, leave them." She hesitated before going on. "I know it sounds preposterous, but I have seen it with my own eyes."

Great-Granny June sat quietly. No one spoke. She considered the words she had heard, turning them over in her mind like a peppermint she would turn over in her mouth. After several moments, she turned her head toward Nick, as best she could. "Is what the girl says true, Nick?"

He tried to fight the huge lump in his throat that almost kept him from being able to answer her. He nodded in assent and said "Yes, Great-Granny June, what Trish says is true. I swear it."

"Then tell me, young man, tell me your story. Tell me when this began. Tell me the circumstances that led up to your discovery of it. Let's think this through together. And pray, son, we have to pray. There is a Power who rules our universe. It seems to me that Power has touched you. Talk to me, young man. Tell me, Nicholas."

He loved hearing her call him Nicholas. His mother had called him that, long ago when she was still living. He wondered how Great-Granny June knew that.

He told her his story and she listened intently. He told her of his trip to the Holy Land, to gather information for an article for his newspaper. He told her that he joined the Christian pilgrims there and walked to Golgotha in his bare feet. He tried to describe to her the wonder and joy and adoration in their faces as they worshiped. He spoke of the small, seemingly insignificant sharp pain in his foot. She listened fascinated and wide-eyed as he told her of the car wreck, the irreparable damage to his leg, and his hospital experience when his leg had been completely healed to the utter amazement of the surgeons. He related the happenings of other healings when he had touched diseased bodies and crippled limbs and they were healed. Nick told her all that was stuck deep in his gut, in his heart and in his soul. He told Great-Granny June, with a trembling voice, that this gift which should bring him only joy was also a torment to him, because he wondered, because he questioned why.

The stillness in the Haven sitting room was almost unearthly. On this usually busy day, all was quiet. By some strange happenstance the three were completely alone. Only the tick of the grandfather clock could be heard as the trio sat silently. Great-Granny June sat with her eyes closed, but Trish and Nick knew she was not sleeping. Her lips moved in silent prayer.

The old sage opened her eyes, looked at Trish and Nick and smiled. She had always been known in the family as the unusual one. She had gifts of her own. She could see things and know things that others could not. She was happy to share those gifts with Nick.

"Yes, yes. I think I can tell you what happened, Nick," she said softly. Somehow I can see it all clearly, and perhaps it is the truth. We will never really know until we are on the other side." Nick and Trish listened, waiting spellbound for her next words.

"Dear young man, you walked on holy ground in Israel. You climbed the rocky hillside that led you to stand on Golgotha where Jesus, the son of God, was crucified nearly two thousand years ago for the sins of all mankind."

"Trish has told me the story, Great-Granny June; that Jesus was born of a virgin in Bethlehem, grew to manhood and healed the sick and lame, was crucified and rose from the dead on the third day, then ascended into heaven to sit at the right hand of God, the Father. He told his people he would return for them someday to take them with him to heaven. Did I get it right, Great-Granny June? It is a new story for me."

"Sounds like you have the facts, Nick. Isn't that what you newspaper men are instructed to find?"

"Yes ma'am, it is. But there is still the big question about what has happened to me."

"Ah, Nick, I think I know. I believe that when you stood on

the sacred grounds of Golgotha, so transformed today from what they used to be, you somehow took a fragment into your foot. A blessed fragment, for I believe it was a tiny piece broken off from one of the spikes that nailed Jesus to the cross. It stayed there through years and years, buried beneath the earth, but working its way up to the surface as years passed. So it was there on the surface the day you visited Golgotha, where you picked it up in the flesh of your foot and it entered into your bloodstream. Now, you have the healing power of Jesus within you, son. God's ways are surely mysterious and so much higher than our ways, we cannot understand them. But for some reason, He chose to give you this gift. I believe that this is the way it has happened, after all these years."

Nick couldn't say a word. He looked at Trish, hoping to take in some of her vibrant strength. He drank in the beauty of her face. Like a rainbow shining through the rain, she was smiling through her tears. They embraced and as they clung to each other, once again this strong, virile young man cried with her. They would know many moments in each other's arms, but none more precious than this.

Nick believed the old woman. It all made sense, as much sense as anything in this world could. And his consciousness, his soul and his spirit opened to the spirit of Jesus at that moment, just as his flesh had opened to the fragment of the spike.

Josephina had come to check on Great Granny June. She felt very protective of her and loved her dearly. She stood quietly watching from the doorway. She did not want to disturb them. She had seen the embrace of the young couple. But now she watched as the young man knelt down and put his arms lovingly around the old one. He held her close for a few silent moments.

But then the silence was broken as Josephina's scream pierced the air and echoed through the Haven halls. She threw her hands high into the air, letting go of the tray that held three Dresden teacups filled with tea. Her hands flew to her mouth in disbelief.

Great-Granny June had stood from her chair to join Nick and Trish in an embrace. She stood as straight and strong as an arrow with her arms around her children, the old and the new. Josephina swayed and had to cling to the door frame to keep from fainting dead away. "How can this be?" she exclaimed to other residents and workers who were gathering now in the parlor. And the din was like the music of the pipes of angels.

Then wise Great-Granny June spoke of what was to come. She asked Nick, "What will the future be for you now, Nick? What of all the others who are sick and infirm and crippled; so many waiting for healing. So many waiting for the great answer that you have found?"

Nick's words echoed through the room. He had said them many times before, but never with the understanding which he now had. For when he spoke, time and all eternity were in his words, "We shall see what we shall see."

CHAPTER 27

THE SERVANT SPINAL Center in Atlanta was bustling inside as it always was by early afternoon. It was not a noisy environment; just nurses and doctors and helpers quietly going about their business of caring for others. What a divine mystery it is that floats in the universe and causes the character of some to be called to medical work. Yet others who work on power lines, sort books in libraries and gather crops for market would never consider such work. And none are so grateful for servant hearts as those who are sick, infirmed and needy.

Dr. Bradford Bowman awoke more anxious than usual to shower and dress, have coffee and toast, and head to his beloved center. In his early waking reverie he remembered that he had a special patient coming in today. He was curious to know what Great-Granny June meant when she said she was coming with a surprise for him today; probably some delicious brownies or cookies as she had made for him before. That would be no surprise, but he would humor her and be delighted with whatever she brought to him. He would gladly participate in her little mystery.

After all, Dr. Bowman liked the mysterious. Science had always held myriad wonders for him. The workings of the human body were a puzzle that he was glad to give his whole life to discovering.

It was his call. The glory, the wonder, the magnificence of the workings of the human body, this all fascinated him. But he found no time in his hurried existence to come to believe in a master creator. He was all science.

Dr. Bowman's mother had long since passed life's scene, and Great-Granny June had become a surrogate mother to him. He could not keep himself from getting emotionally involved with this dear old, pain-wracked, bent over person. The truth be told, he loved her as one of his favorite patients, and he longed to do more for her pitiful misshapen body. In his eyes, she was beautiful. But he could only keep a check on her from time to time when her great granddaughter brought her in for the therapy that was available to her. Each time he was in her presence he realized that it was not her radiant soul that was crippled, but only her frail body. Yes, considered Dr. Bradford Bowman, there is something almost magical about Great Granny June.

The doctor worked diligently through his morning hours, managed to get a quick bite to eat for lunch and more coffee to fuel his afternoon. When he did manage to get a quiet moment to himself, he thought of Great-Granny June and smiled. He glanced at his watch. Her appointment was at two o'clock. "Almost time," he said aloud to the corridor walls. He took the time to check his appearance for he wanted to be at his best for her. She always called him her handsome doctor and he loved this small stroke of his ego.

He heard a bustle of noise in the waiting room. The voices of the staff there seemed lively and excited, somewhat like a gaggle of waddling geese that had suddenly been disturbed. He entered the waiting room and stood stock still, staring at the unbelievable sight which greeted him. "Great-Granny June," he stammered. "What—what has happened to you?"

The watchers in the room were quiet, now, in honor of Great-Granny June. She stood tall and straight, and reached her slender arms out to her doctor and friend. He took her hands and gazed into her wistful eyes which had beheld so much of history in her many years. He was overcome and she reached up to wipe away a single tear that had escaped from his eye. He heard her say in her scratchy, ancient voice, "God is good, my dear doctor. God is good."

After a bit of happy conversation from all around, the strong doctor regained his professional bearing and gave direction again. "Great-Granny June, will you please come to my examining room? My, you certainly did have a mysterious surprise for me. I am anxious to delve into the circumstances."

"Of course, my handsome doctor," she said with a twinkle in her eye. "But I have a request. May my four friends come with me, and the baby, too, just this once? I'd like to introduce them to you, and have them join in our celebratory time together."

"Well, I suppose it couldn't matter just this time, my dear girl. This is a special time, after all."

"Oh, how I love hearing you call me 'girl', Doctor Bowman," Great-Granny June quipped.

The entourage of friends, Kathy and Bruce Louis, now married, accompanied by their beautiful baby girl, Esther, along with Trish and Nick, had decided to make this trip to hear what the doctor had to say after Trish told Kathy about the amazing miracle that had happened with Great-Granny June. The group began a jaunty walk down the hospital hallway. Their laughter and chatter rang in the air and echoed back to those left behind like the clappers of sterling bells.

They passed several doors, most of them closed to the hall to honor the privacy of the patient inside. Suddenly Great-Granny June motioned for them to be quiet. "Listen. Listen, everyone," she commanded sweetly and everyone obeyed. Her finger went to her lips and motioned for everyone to be silent. "Shhhh," she instructed gently. They stood quietly, straining to hear what Great-Granny June had discovered.

"Oh, what a sweet voice," crooned Great Granny June. "Listen. Can you hear her voice? Listen."

The group looked in the door and saw her then, a wisp of a young girl in a tidy blue dress, sitting on a stool beside the bed of a man. She held a small book in her hand with brightly colored pictures in watercolor, a child's Bible story book. She was reading to the frail man in the bed, obviously confined for some time, although he appeared fairly young. "He maketh me to lie down in green pastures. He leadeth me beside the still waters. He restoreth my soul."

And as the 9-year-old girl continued, Great-Granny June's loved ones could see the matriarch's lips moving with hers in perfect synergy, "He leads me in the paths of righteousness for his namesake. Yea, though I walk through the valley of the shadow of death, I will fear no evil, for thou art with me. Psalm 23."

"Oh, hello there," spoke the precocious girl, as she caught sight of them at the door. "Oh, a baby! I love babies. Won't you come in? My friend won't mind. I was just reading to him as I do when I come for therapy day each week. You see, he can't hold a book for himself." Her voice became very quiet then, as if it was just too sad a thing to say out loud. "He is paralyzed from the neck down. He had a terrible accident in a swimming pool a few months ago."

Kathy's eyes were on the doctor. She looked hesitantly at him with a question on her face. This was all such a strange circumstance. But then, there had been many strange happenings recently in her life. Dr. Bowman nodded yes as if he had been given some infinite cue. Kathy came into the room with her husband and her baby and the couple stood one on either side of the young reader. The girl declared with joy, "Oh, what a beautiful baby." And the parents smiled and were glad they came into the room. Dr. Bowman indicated for Trish and Nick to come in, too. They stood on the far side of the crippled patient's bed. Dr. Bowman brought Great-Granny June in to join them. They stood at the foot of the patient's bed. Kathy was occupied with her baby girl, as she was getting a little fussy and she didn't want her to disturb the patient.

Dr. Bowman spoke and introduced the little girl. "This

delightful sprite is my patient, Natalie. She took a terrific tumble from her bicycle. We are treating her spine. We are working on it, but we have not been able as yet to relieve her pain."

"Oh, doctor, it's not so bad. I can take it," she said. Her cheerful spirit shone in her eyes. "Everyone has some kind of trouble." And with wisdom beyond her years she added, "There are lots of people much worse off than I am." But they saw her wince as she turned back to the man lying prone on the bed beside her. The friendly elfin girl reached out to each of them in turn, shaking hands, first Kathy and then her kind husband, then on to all the rest as if she were a politician running for office. She took the time to warmly coo to the now sleeping baby in Kathy's arms. Great-Granny June was not left out as Natalie acknowledged her with a sincere and welcoming hug. Nick was standing tall and silently taking in the scene. He saw the painful movements that she tried to hide as she moved around the room. At last her little hand was in his. As her green eyes edged with gold looked deeply into Nick's beckoning eyes, her face took on a puzzled look of wonder. Her hand was stilled and she seemed frozen there, holding tightly to Nick's hand for a long pause. Nick placed his free hand on her upturned head and stroked her hair gently. She didn't seem to mind that this stranger was touching her; rather, she felt comforted and happy when he touched her. And her spine felt strangely warmed.

The tranquil and mysterious spell between the two of them was suddenly broken when they heard Kathy gasp. Her whole body was trembling, and to the amazement of everyone, she became engulfed in deep, heartfelt sobs. Bruce was aware that her knees had gone weak, and he quickly reached for her. Trish quickly took the baby. Kathy turned and fled from the room and stopped to lean against the wall outside lest she fall into a heap on the hospital floor. Little Natalie was bewildered. Great-Granny June took her hand and put her finger to her lips once again to indicate for Natalie to be silent. "It's all right, Natalie, dear," she said firmly with gentle command in her voice; and somehow Natalie knew at that moment that all would be well.

The professor was beside his wife in a millisecond, cradling her in his strong arms. He could not imagine what was happening. No one could.

"Kathy," he pleaded, "Tell me, darling, what is wrong? Can you tell me, Kathy?" He was beside himself with worry for this beautiful woman he loved so much.

Kathy tried to speak, but the words choked in her throat. It was as if it was some horror movie that she had never seen suddenly played before her eyes. Finally a name came from deep inside her throat, a wretched guttural sound that at first was only a pianissimo, then as it was repeated and repeated, it climbed to a shriek of torment as she shouted, "Hammond. Hammond James. It's Hammond James!" And her sobbing began anew as she clung fiercely to her husband.

The clock on the wall ticked only a bare three seconds until the truth hit home to the professor. He groaned and could hardly believe that it was now Kathy's fate to meet the monster who had betrayed her. "Oh, my poor dear," he spoke softly, longing to comfort her and not knowing how he possibly could. "Is it really possible, Kathy? Are you sure? Is this Hammond lying paralyzed in the cool, white room next to us?" He had often imagined Hammond in pits of mud with hogs about him, or burning in the fires of hell, but never had he imagined him as they had found him here. But here he was, this evil bit of garbage that had taken away her innocence, harming his Kathy so cruelly. Yet she had a beautiful baby girl as a result of his treachery, and they both adored her.

Trish and Nick came into the hall to stand with their friends. They were familiar with the details of the terrible event in Kathy's life. When they had heard Kathy screaming his name, they had looked again at the pitiful, emaciated figure in the hospital bed. It was hard to make him out from the man he had been. But Trish could vaguely see a bare reflection of the strikingly handsome preacher she had heard speak so eloquently. He was a ghost of himself.

"Hammond James?" Nick breathed the question into the sterile air, and his heart ached when Kathy nodded and spoke a barely audible, "Yes."

Great-Granny June, too, knew the story of the tragic events that had brought Bruce and Kathy to this point in their lives. She grieved for Kathy, but rejoiced at the gift of the baby they had been given to love. Her intangible gift of wisdom allowed her to perceive the weaving of the tangled threads of past heartbreak into a beautiful tapestry of the present. Though it was beyond their understanding, she knew beyond the shadow of a doubt that they all had a divine appointment for this particular day.

She still held Natalie's hand, but released it to take her creaky old bones, now straight as a Georgia pine, to her family in the hall. She lovingly pried Kathy from her husband's embrace. Everyone always seemed to obey Great-Granny June. She stroked Kathy's still trembling arm and hand with her comforting fingers and Kathy was calmed.

Great-Granny June spoke and all listened intently. "Oh, sweet daughter of the ruler of the universe, I know you must hurt terribly. But don't you see, child, a mighty God has brought us together, all of us, in this place, at this specific time. And he is in the midst of us. We are never alone. He shares our pain and he shares our joy and he numbers the hairs of our heads."

Great-Granny June then gently tugged on Kathy's arm. She cajoled her with her with her irresistible smile and a nod of her grey-wispy-crowned head. She said only one word. "Come."

There was no need of further conversation. The lines of the play had long ago been written, and now it was but for the players to enact their part in this story of destiny. Silently they all entered the room where Hammond James lay. One by one they encircled his bed. The wasted and pathetic skeleton of a man who lay there was the only soul who spoke. He recognized Kathy. He always remembered her as his prize, the most radiant of all the flowers he had crushed and bruised. That was a part of his torment. His mind was still in working condition, though his body was useless. He remembered his past all too vividly and had only hours upon hours for regret.

They heard him whimper like a poor animal that had been whipped by a cruel master. He looked imploringly at Kathy who stood bravely now beside his bed. His eyes held her captive as he begged her to forgive him. "I—I'm sorry," was all he could say.

There was an interminable pause as everyone waited, hardly daring to breathe. At last Kathy, heroine and leading lady, picked up her cue. She made one small, dramatic movement. It was simply a nod to her good friend, Nick. It was only Nick who read the silent movement of her mouth as her lips formed the words, "Help him."

All stood at salutatory attention in the room. Only Nick moved. He came close to Hammond James, or Ralph Jones, or whatever his name was. It didn't matter anymore. Nick bent over the infirmed man's body, his chest resting on Hammond's torso. Nick stretched his right hand and arm toward Hammond's head; his left pointed down to his feet.

The scientific and learned doctor Bowman watched fascinated. He was aware deep inside himself that it was alright to submit his patient to this young man. Someone, some power had helped Great-Granny June. Perhaps--he couldn't believe what his scientific mind was considering at this moment.

A low, growling moan pierced the stillness of the room; and soon there was another. Almost imperceptibly at first, Hammond's leg twitched under Nick's outstretched arm. "God help me," sobbed Hammond James aloud as he moved his other leg. "Oh, Jesus, help me," he cried, as he screamed out the name of the Galilean he had so many times taken in vain. "What is happening to me?"

Hammond's arms began to flail and move about and Nick

knew his work was done. He raised his body to an upright position and stood and took a place beside Trish. He, above all the others, was amazed at the miracles which had passed through him. He would never get used to the wonder of it. The baby cried. The intensity of the moment was broken, and such a chatter and clatter of joy was heard as never before in the Servant Spinal Center.

Dr. Bowman quieted a laughing and sobbing Hammond. "Now, take it easy there, son. Let's give it some time. You must be careful." By now Hammond had swung his legs off his bed and would have sprung up if the doctor had not chided and calmed him.

"A little child shall lead them," reads a prophecy of old, and Natalie did. She laughed and cheered and she jumped up and down with only the exuberance that a child can muster. And the good doctor once more had to correct his patient. "Natalie, you must not do more damage to your back."

The little girl smiled at the kind doctor, who was as astounded and confused as the others in the room. She struck a delightful pose with her hands on hips and looked one by one at each astonished soul in this blessed room. "Oh, no, Dr. Bowman. Don't you understand? My pain is all gone. It doesn't hurt at all!"

Nick pulled Trish to him, placing his arms lovingly around her. Their eyes met. All the missing pieces came together now. With unspeakable joy on their faces and tears in their eyes, Nick and Trish simultaneously embraced their future; to surrender their lives together without reservation to a Galilean named Jesus who had chosen them for a miraculous life-long journey.

Natalie looked at each person in the room, cocked her curly-haired head to one side and said in unison with all the invisible angels in the room, "I think maybe a miracle has happened here."

CPSIA information can be obtained
at www.ICGtesting.com
Printed in the USA
LVHW090413210220
647535LV00001B/27